EXTRA! EXTRA!
READ ALL ABOUT IT!

They're all here in one unbeatable volume: the
players, the teams, the coaches, and the fans
who made football fumbles—and history.
You'll never find another lineup this wacky:
The Funniest Debuts, The Worst Teams of All
Time, The Most Inept Kicking Performances,
The Tackiest Tackles Ever Made, The Zaniest
Pep Talks Ever Delivered, The Weakest
Defensive Performances, The Wackiest
Fumbles, and, yes . . . more! in . . .

THE FOOTBALL HALL OF SHAME™
YOUNG FANS' EDITION

THE FOOTBALL HALL OF SHAME™

YOUNG FANS' EDITION

BRUCE NASH AND ALLAN ZULLO
BERNIE WARD, CURATOR

AN ARCHWAY PAPERBACK
Published by POCKET BOOKS
New York   London   Toronto   Sydney   Tokyo

An Archway Paperback published by
POCKET BOOKS, a division of Simon & Schuster Inc.
1230 Avenue of the Americas, New York, NY 10020

ISBN: 0-671-69197-X

First Archway Paperback printing November 1989

10 9 8 7 6 5 4 3 2

THE FOOTBALL HALL OF SHAME is a registered
trademark of Nash and Zullo Productions, Inc.

AN ARCHWAY PAPERBACK and colophon are
registered trademarks of Simon & Schuster Inc.

Printed in the U.S.A.

IL 5+

To Sophie, Robyn, and Jenny Nash
and Kathy, Allison, and Sasha Zullo,
our greatest cheerleaders

ACKNOWLEDGMENTS

We wish to thank all the fans, players, coaches, and sportswriters who contributed nominations.

We are especially grateful to those players and coaches, past and present, who shared a few laughs with us as they recalled the moments that earned them a place in The Football Hall of SHAME.

This book couldn't have been completed without the outstanding research of Al Kermisch, or the kindness of Ernest Clevenger, president of Faulkner University, and Dick Cohen, president of the Sports Bookshelf in Ridgefield, Connecticut, both of whom allowed us access to their wonderful collections of football books. We wish to thank Donna Dupuy for her fine editing.

We also appreciate the special efforts of Joe Horrigan and Ann Mangus of The Pro Football Hall of Fame in Canton, Ohio; Bob Carroll, president of the Professional Football Researchers Association; Bob Kirlin, president of the College Football Researchers Association; Tim Williams, of the NFL Alumni Association; Lana Thompson and Eleanor Arnold.

In addition, we want to thank all the sportswriters, sports information directors, librarians, archivists, and fans who provided us with needed information and material. Special thanks go to: Brad Angers, Jim Campbell, George Castle, Loren Chamberlain, Larry Dale, Glenn Fess, Jim Ford, Frank Garofalo, Joe Gordon, Ellie Harness, Jamie Kimbrough, Larry Landman, Glen Miller, Dave Pellitier, Helen Ryan, Marc Ryan, Bill Whitmore, and Robert M. Willingham, Jr.

CONTENTS

CONTENTS

THE
FOOTBALL
HALL
OF SHAME ™

YOUNG FANS'
EDITION

KICKING OFF

For nearly a century, football's swivel-hipped runners, golden-armed passers, clean-cut all-Americans, and undefeated conference champions have been praised. But let's face it, winners and heroes are *boring!* The things that really make the game so fun, exciting, and entertaining are the muffed handoffs, the dropped passes, the shanked punts, and the missed blocks.

Until now, the fumblers, bumblers, and stumblers have escaped the spotlight. They hid their shame in the huddle. But no longer. We have their numbers—and a place for each of them in The Football Hall of SHAME.

Fans have given us lots of nominations. Our own research has uncovered many more little-known zany incidents. Hilarious happenings have occurred in college football, the National Football League, and the former World Football League.

After going through all the nominations, we selected those that had the best chance of making it into the Hall. Then we checked the accuracy of these accounts by reading record books, historical material, and newspaper microfilm at the Football Hall of Fame in Canton, Ohio, and the Library of Congress in Washington,

D.C. We also were helped by the Professional Football Researchers Association. The sports information directors and librarians at various colleges gave us help, too. When possible, we conducted personal interviews with the nominees themselves.

Just what does it mean to be in The Football Hall of SHAME? It's a special honor of a moment we can all identify with—and laugh about—because each of us has fouled up at one time or another. We have fun with both the superstars and the bozos. As our motto says: "Fame *and* shame are part of the game."

FIRST DOWNERS

Rookies dream about what glory their first game will bring. They see themselves blasting through the line for the winning touchdown in the final seconds. They imagine leaping high in the air for the game-saving interception. That's the fantasy. The reality is that in their debuts, they often disgrace themselves completely. Sometimes the memory stays with them the rest of their careers—which can be a whole lot shorter than they planned. For "The Funniest Debuts," The Football Hall of SHAME inducts the following:

LEON HART

End ■ Notre Dame Fighting Irish ■ Sept. 28, 1946

In Leon Hart's first game in a Notre Dame uniform, he displayed the raw power that later made him an All-America and a Heisman Trophy winner.

Leon Hart makes a knockout debut.

He drove forward with his head down and flattened the man in front of him. Unfortunately, the man was teammate Bob Livingstone, and Hart knocked him unconscious.

Summoned by coach Frank Leahy midway through a game against Illinois, the wide-eyed Hart listened eagerly. "Leon, you're only a 17-year-old freshman," Leahy said. "This is your first game and I expect you to be nervous. You're up against older, more experienced opponents. But remember, if I didn't have confidence in you, I wouldn't send you into the game. Now, get in there at right end for Zilly."

The supercharged youth headed full throttle for the huddle. He crashed smack into Livingstone, a halfback who was returning to the bench for a rest. Livingstone went down in a heap.

When he was revived a few minutes later, Livingstone shook his aching head. He said, "I've never been hit that hard before. That kid's going to be all right."

"Yeah," agreed Notre Dame trainer Hughie Burns, applying a bandage to Livingstone's chin. "But first we gotta teach him whose side he's on."

GEORGE CONNOR

Tackle-Linebacker ■ Chicago Bears ■ 1948–55

George Connor was a little slow to understand why his early days in pro football were so painful. Opposing linemen kept belting him in the jaw. Eventually, though, those punches knocked some sense into the rookie.

George Connor gets some sense knocked into him.
UPI/BETTMANN NEWSPHOTOS

In his first few pro games, Connor was the backup tackle for Fred Davis. Whenever Davis needed a rest, he would raise his hand in the huddle. That was the signal for Connor to replace him after the next play.

Connor's first taste of life in the NFL came during an exhibition game. When Davis' arm went up, Connor grabbed his helmet and watched the end of the play. Then he raced onto the field. On his first play from scrimmage, he was promptly punched in the mouth by the opposing lineman. Although it hurt, Connor thought that maybe this was the typical welcome for rookies.

Later in the game, Connor again replaced Davis. He set up against a different lineman. But the results were the same. Once again, he got socked in the face.

"It was the same story during those first few games," Connor, now a Hall of Famer, recalled. "Every time I went in the game, the guy opposite me smashed me in the mouth. I thought maybe they didn't like me personally, or maybe they didn't like rookies from Notre Dame. I was afraid that if this was the way pro football was played, I wasn't sure I wanted to keep playing."

Finally, early in his fifth game, Connor wised up. This time, when Davis raised his hand, Connor kept his eyes on Davis instead of the play. When the ball was snapped, he saw Davis lunge across the line, punch the opposing lineman in the face, and trot off toward the Bears' bench. It was then that Connor realized he was paying for all of Davis' dirty work.

"The linemen didn't pay any attention to who was opposite them," recalled Connor. "They were just mad that somebody had punched them. So from that moment on, whenever I substituted for Davis, I'd tell the opposing lineman, 'Fred Davis out, George Connor in.' I never got hit again.

"After that game, I asked Fred why he was doing that to me. He just laughed in my face and said, 'Why did it take you five games to catch on?' "

REX KEELING

Punter ■ Cincinnati Bengals ■ Dec. 1, 1968

Rex Keeling's debut as a Bengal punter was so pitiful that coach Paul Brown cut him at halftime.

Keeling was in Alabama selling cars for his father when he got a call from Brown. The Bengals' regular punter, Dale Livingston, had just been called up for military duty. The team needed a punter for the final three games of the season. Keeling had tried out for the Bengals as a free agent the summer before. He jumped at the chance to play pro football.

He should have stayed in the car business.

Although he hadn't punted in months, Keeling booted 50-yarders during practice the week before his first game. But he kicked for barely half that distance in his pro debut against the Boston Patriots. Keeling averaged only 28.3 yards on six punts—and had one partially blocked.

His most shameful moment came late in the second quarter. On a fake punt at midfield, he bobbled the snap. Then he tried to run with the ball. Finally, he threw it forward underhanded. It fell to the ground and was ruled a fumble.

Boston took possession on the Cincinnati 45-yard line. Keeling's bungle set up a touchdown for the Patriots, who led 26–0 at halftime.

In the locker room, Brown was furious. He blasted Keeling for letting the pressure of the pros get to him. "This game is just too big for you, Rex," he snarled in front of the team. "You just can't handle it. You're

8

gone!" With that, Brown turned to his son Mike, a team executive, and said, "Write this boy out a check for what we owe him." Then, loud enough for all to hear, Brown muttered, "That's what I get for trying to make a kicker out of a used-car salesman."

In recalling his brief pro career, Keeling said he had a feeling Brown was fed up with him when he called for the fake punt. "I couldn't find anybody open so I took off, and this 300-pound monster caught me and knocked me into a TV camera and almost killed me," said Keeling. "I've always believed Brown called that play just to get even with me."

ROSE BOWL

Jan. 1, 1902

The first Rose Bowl game was such a mismatch that the losing team quit. They gave up with eight minutes left to play. Red-faced officials were so embarrassed they didn't stage another Rose Bowl for fourteen years.

The oldest post-season Bowl started in 1902 as part of Pasadena's annual Rose Festival. The Stanford Cardinal team was selected to represent the West. Their opponent was the eastern powerhouse, the Michigan Wolverines. The Wolverines were awesome. They had won all 11 of their games—and shut out every opponent. Along the way, they racked up an incredible 555 points. Their defense was just as tough. The longest gain against Michigan all year was only 15 yards.

Clearly, the weaker, smaller Stanford team did not belong on the same field. The snarling Wolverines injured enough Cardinal players to fill a hospital ward. "We couldn't stand the terrific smashing of those bulldog fighters," said Stanford trainer "Dad" Moulton. "After they had laid out our best men, they had everything their own way."

Michigan had bulldozed its way to a 49–0 lead halfway into the fourth quarter. The Cardinal players didn't need college degrees to know when enough was enough. Actually, 49–0 was more than enough.

With eight minutes remaining, Stanford captain R. S. Fisher staggered over to Michigan captain Hugh White. He said, "If you are willing, we are ready to quit." White, a brutal left tackle, showed some compassion for the first time all day. White said that was fine and dandy with him.

The Tournament of Roses Association was mortified. They decided to drop football from the annual program—until California produced a team that wouldn't shame the West.

So what replaced football during the annual Rose Festival? Believe it or not, they ran chariot races! Amateur drivers nearly killed each other, so professional drivers took over. Then the cry of "fix" tainted the races.

The Tournament of Roses Association finally decided that football wasn't so bad after all. In 1916, after memories of its awful debut had faded, football returned to the Rose Bowl.

THE BOTTOM OF
THE BARREL

It's a good thing that losing, cellar-dwelling teams don't have postage stamps made of them. People wouldn't know which side to spit on. These teams don't belong on the gridiron. They belong in a Three Stooges movie. For "The Worst Teams of All Time," The Football Hall of SHAME inducts the following:

DALLAS TEXANS

1952

The Dallas Texans were an NFL joke—a very bad joke.

With a roster of wide-eyed greenhorns and broken-down old hands, they were saddled with a legacy of failure. Halfway through their first and only season, they were kicked out of town. Forced to wander the league as vagabonds, they disbanded at year's end. They were the last NFL team to fold.

The Texans were the offspring of losers—the New York Yanks. That team lost so many games and dollars for owner Ted Collins that he gave the franchise back to the NFL. A few weeks later, commissioner Bert Bell awarded the franchise to Texas millionaire Giles Miller. Texas had long been a hotbed for college and high school football. Declared Miller, "There is room enough in Texas for all kinds of football." But not bad football.

Only 17,499 curious spectators attended the opening day game. They watched the New York Giants welcome the Texans to the league with a 24–6 defeat. The fans had seen more than enough. The Cotton Bowl turned into an empty echo chamber during the next three home games. Unable to meet his financial obligations, Miller returned control of the team to the league.

The squad was moved to Hershey, Pennsylvania, where it held loosely organized practices. For the rest of the year, the Texans traveled the country as a homeless road team.

They drew more flies than fans, losing 11 of 12 games. They averaged only 15 points per game, but gave up a whopping 35 points per game. They finished last in total yards, and missed 7 of 27 PATs, as well as all four field goal attempts.

Coach Jim Phelan had no luck with the kicking game. He tried turning college passing star Don Klosterman into a kicking specialist. Unfortunately, Klosterman missed a field goal and was cut the next day. Before leaving, Klosterman claimed he deserved another chance. Later, when the team reviewed the game film, Phelan stopped the projector after Klosterman's failed kick. The coach backed up the reel and ran the play over again. "There," he told his players. "Who says I didn't give Klosterman a second chance?"

Another reason the team stunk was that Phelan hated practice as much as the players did. One day they ran a few plays without fouling up. Phelan stopped practice, loaded everybody on a bus, and took them to the racetrack.

The Texans' only win ever came at the expense of the Chicago Bears. It was in Akron, Ohio, of all places. The game was billed as the second part of a Thanksgiving doubleheader. In the morning game, two high school teams played to a full house. Before the start of the pro contest, almost everyone went home.

Looking over the few fans in the stands, Phelan told his troops, "Instead of running under the goal posts for introductions, let's just go up and shake hands with everybody. It would be faster. It won't take more than a minute or two."

Chicago coach George Halas took the Texans for patsies. He played his second stringers until the Bears trailed 20–2. The Texans held on for a shocking 27–23 victory.

Flushed with success, the Texans prepared for their next opponent, the Philadelphia Eagles. Not wanting to be upset, Eagle coach Greasy Neale sent a scout to watch the Texans practice in Hershey. When the scout returned, he told Neale, "You're not going to believe this, but they were playing volleyball over the goal posts." The Texans reverted to form and lost 38–21 to the Eagles. In their very last game, the Texans were trounced 41–6 by the Detroit Lions. When they scored their only touchdown, it was late in the game. But Phelan shouted, "We've got them on the run now!"

At the end of the season, half the Texans—twenty

players—quit pro football. Among them were nine rookies who wished they had stayed in college. Twelve others went to the league's newest franchise, the Baltimore Colts. Lamented Phelan, "We got all the breaks—and they were all bad."

MACALESTER COLLEGE SCOTS

1974–80

The Macalester Scots twisted coaching great Vince Lombardi's philosophy inside out. To them losing wasn't everything; it was the only thing.

Like an unoiled engine misfiring on all cylinders, Macalester sputtered to 50 straight losses. They set a National Collegiate Athletic Association record for failure. The school did one better than its famous alumnus, Walter Mondale. He lost 49 out of 50 states in the 1984 Presidential election.

Like Mondale, the Scots didn't just lose. They lost big. In 1977, they dropped all eight games by a combined point total of 532–39. They were blown away by such scores as 62–7, 46–0, 51–7, and 55–13.

Macalester is a small liberal arts school in St. Paul, Minnesota. Its 1,700 students are known for academic excellence. The team it fielded was battered and bruised mentally and physically. They should have changed the school colors to black and blue. Most of the players were freshmen and sophomores. Macalester's juniors and seniors were either too hurt, too discouraged, or too smart to keep playing.

Others stuck it out as the losses piled up like autumn leaves. Some guys had played four full seasons without ever taking a halftime lead into the locker room. And with each embarrassing setback, the pressure grew, as did media attention.

"It was so bad," recalled coach Tom Hosier, "that in a scrimmage against a junior college, we went in the huddle on offense and I thought we'd never come out of it. We were that afraid to lose."

Their best offensive play was downing the kickoff in the end zone. At least it gained 20 yards every time. Occasionally, they tried a surprise play—like running up the middle on first down. Sometimes the Scots caught their opponents off guard and racked up a yard or two.

There was talk at the school of dropping football. After all, the team's running backs had been doing that with regularity for several years. But then came Macalester's biggest game ever.

On October 28, 1978, they faced St. John's of Collegeville, Minnesota. The nation watched and held its breath. With one more loss, the Scots could break the old NCAA record of 39 straight defeats. The movement on campus to scrap football in favor of soccer—or anything else—was forgotten. About 3,000 excited, sign-waving fans showed up at Macalester Stadium for the historic event. Banners proclaimed, "We're No. 1" and "Go Big Mac" and warned Notre Dame to watch out.

In the first quarter, the Scots recovered a fumble and then completed a third-down pass. The fans began shouting "Orange Bowl! Orange Bowl! Orange Bowl!"

But St. John's Mark McCullen ran 72 yards for a touchdown. A Macalester defender had a shot at stop-

ping McCullen near the 10-yard line. He was neatly—
and unwittingly—blocked by an official who did not
see him coming.

Macalester's longest run of the day occurred when
the campus dog, a two-year-old mongrel, scampered
onto the field. That was also the play that brought the
biggest cheer.

The Scots were clobbered 44–0, and the record was
theirs—possibly forever. Despite the rout, it was clear
that the Macalester defense had grown stronger. The
year before, St. John's had beaten the Scots 70–0.

With every loss following the St. John's whipping,
Macalester hit a new record low. But we all wake up
from nightmares. For Macalester, the nightmare ended
on September 6, 1980, against Mount Scenario College
of Ladysmith, Wisconsin.

With 11 seconds left, the score was tied at 14–14.
Scots freshman kicker Bob Kaye was sent in to boot a
23-yard field goal. His kick wobbled through the goal
post and skimmed the left upright. But neatness
doesn't count. The kick was good. The Macalester
Scots had won a football game. The 50-game losing
streak was over.

"There were parties all over campus," recalled athletic director Dennis Keihn. "We had champagne on
ice for the occasion. Trouble is, it had been on ice for
six years."

Coach Tom Hosier was asked what the team would
do for an encore. He declared, "Win again next week!"
After one victory, overconfidence had already set in.

It would have been nice to report that the Scots went
on to win two in a row. But they lost their next game
20–7, halting their one-game winning streak. It had to
end sometime . . . but so soon?

TAMPA BAY BUCCANEERS

1976–77

No professional football team started out more miserably than the Bucs. They lost their first 26 regular season games—11 by shutout.

The Bucs were headed in the wrong direction even before the kickoff of their debut. After their pre-game warmups in the Houston Astrodome, they followed their coach, John McKay, off the field. They followed him into the concrete innards of the stadium, where they promptly got lost.

Forty-five players, eight coaches, equipment men, trainers, and doctors wandered around. They searched in vain for their locker room. Finally, a security guard found the Bucs and led them to their quarters. But by then, the Bucs had just a few minutes to get ready for the kickoff. As it turned out, the offense stayed lost; it never found the end zone. The Bucs mustered a mere 108 yards in a 20–0 loss to the Houston Oilers.

The next week, the offense produced just 13 yards through the air. "The running backs ran like they were mud fences," complained McKay. Tampa Bay either failed to move the football or was thrown for a loss 39 times in that game.

The Bucs didn't make their first touchdown until their fourth game. When they did, it was scored by the defense on a 44-yard fumble recovery. Most of the Bucs' offensive punch was supplied by cornerback Mike Washington. He threw a fist and was thrown out

17

of the game. Afterward, McKay said, "We will be back. Maybe not in this century, but we will be back."

McKay lost his patience and temper after their eighth straight loss, 28–19 to Kansas City. He thundered, "They were absolutely horrible, and that's the nicest thing I can say about them."

The next week, Tampa Bay raised the hopes of its fans. The Bucs tied Denver 10–10 in the third quarter. But the joy was short-lived. The Bucs lost 48–13, and McKay's frustration reached its peak. He refused to shake Denver coach John Ralston's hand after the game. Instead, McKay accused Ralston of running up the score.

The following week was even worse. The New York Jets sacked Buc quarterbacks four times. Taking advantage of six turnovers, New York won its first shutout in thirteen years, 34–0.

In the Bucs' final game that year, they were clobbered 31–14 by the New England Patriots. That made them the only NFL expansion team ever to go winless in its first season. "I'll probably take a little time off," said a weary McKay, "and go hide someplace."

The Bucs' second year started off just like their first. In their first four games they scored only one touchdown. They lost for the second straight year to their expansion brothers, the Seattle Seahawks. This time, the score was 30–23, including 4 interceptions and 2 fumbles. The Bucs' offense scored its most points ever, but the defense took the day off.

The next week, the Bucs lost to Green Bay, 13 to terrible. Said the local newspaper: "The Tampa Bay Bucs pulled out all the stops to ward off an impending win, and kept their losing streak intact. The Bucs used timely penalties, fumbles, mental lapses, and an absolutely pointless display of offensive football to further secure their position at the bottom of the NFL barrel."

They played rookies so inexperienced that some of them hadn't even lettered. Fans began hoping for 0-for-forever. They wore T-shirts that read "Go for 0," and cheered the visiting teams. They had little reason to cheer the Bucs. But on occasion they would applaud when the team did something exciting—like making a particularly smooth entry onto the field.

Finally, 1,298 days after the Bucs were awarded an NFL franchise, they tasted victory.

On December 11, 1977, the laughingstocks of the league won their very first game. It was a 33–14 romp over the hapless New Orleans Saints. Nothing could have been worse for New Orleans. "What a nightmare!" declared Hank Stram, coach of the bedeviled Saints. "It's the worst experience of my coaching career. We're ashamed of our people, our fans, our organization."

SICK KICKS

Kickers think of themselves as game-win-
ners who carry the fate of their teams on
their talented toes. But sometimes their for-
tunes are more like bad punts—shanked out
of bounds. To the lousy kicker, hang time
means how long it will take for angry fans to
lynch him. The coffin corner is where they
want to bury him. For "The Most Inept
Kicking Performances," The Football Hall
of SHAME inducts the following:

MIKE CLARK

Placekicker ■ Dallas Cowboys ■ Dec. 28, 1969

Mike Clark was responsible for the most embarrassing
kickoff ever witnessed in an NFL play-off game.

Late in the game, the Cowboys scored a touchdown,
but still trailed the Cleveland Browns 38–7. They decided to try an onside kick to get the ball back.

The front line of the Browns tensed up, waiting for
the short kick. Meantime, the Cowboys eagerly waited

to pounce on the pigskin. Clark knew he had to hit it just right. He had to squib it so it would travel at least 10 yards—but not much farther. With total concentration, he trotted toward the ball and planted his left foot. Then he swung with his right.

The Cowboys charged forward and banged into the Browns. While some of the players blocked, others surged to where the ball should have gone. But it wasn't there. A frantic search began. No, it wasn't under a pile of Browns or a gang of Cowboys. When the players finally spotted the ball, it was standing upright, where Clark had placed it. It was still on the kicking tee. Clark had whiffed the kick!

His shoulders hunched, Clark just stood over the ball for a moment. The Dallas boo-birds—already upset over the score—hooted and jeered. Clark shook his head.

The Cowboys were penalized 5 yards for being offside so Clark tried another onside kick. This time he managed to kick the ball, and both teams dove for it. But all the smashing helmets, hurling bodies, and clawing fingers were pointless. Clark's kick hadn't gone the required distance. Once again, Dallas was penalized 5 yards.

By now, Clark could feel the heat steaming off the necks of his angry teammates. He sure wasn't going to mess up his third straight kickoff attempt. This time he had a foolproof plan. He ran up to the ball and booted it deep.

Clark was later dishonored by the Dallas Bonehead Club for this pitiful kicking performance. At the award ceremonies, he scolded himself by saying, "Everyone is entitled to make a mistake, but not in front of 70,000 spectators and a national TV audience."

RAFAEL SEPTIEN

Placekicker ■ Los Angeles Rams–Dallas Cowboys
1977–85

Rafael Septien has no equal—when it comes to lamebrained excuses for missed field goals.

His alibis are as weak as a squib off the crossbar. And they're as weird as a hot pink goalpost.

Against the Houston Oilers on September 29, 1985, he muffed 4 of 5 field goal attempts. But Septien didn't

Rafael Septien blows another field goal.
AP/WIDE WORLD PHOTOS

rely on old excuses like "It was a bad snap" or "The holder messed up." Nope, Septien put the blame squarely on his own shoulders. He confessed, "I was too busy reading my stats on the scoreboard."

Later, when he blew a field goal in a game at Texas Stadium, Septien had another reason ready: "The grass was too tall." So was his tale of woe. Texas Stadium doesn't even have grass. Its surface is artificial turf.

Once when he shanked a chip shot, he said it was because "the 30-second clock distracted me." Another time, he booted a wounded duck that fell far short of the uprights. His excuse: "My helmet was too tight and it was squeezing my brain. I couldn't think."

Septien has seldom blamed anyone else for his messed-up kicks. But he did once, when yet another field goal attempt went wide. Turning to his holder, quarterback Danny White, he said, "No wonder. You placed the ball upside down."

CLAIR SCOTT

Punter ■ Indiana Hoosiers ■ Nov. 8, 1913

Punters tend to get angry at themselves when a kick falls harmlessly into the opponent's end zone for a touchback. They should thank their lucky shoelaces they never suffered the fate of Clair Scott.

He booted the worst punt in football history.

Scott's moment of shame came during the Iowa Hawkeyes' 60–0 trouncing of his Hoosiers. Late in the second quarter, the Hoosiers faced a fourth down on

Clair Scott booted the worst punt in college history.
INDIANA UNIVERSITY ATHLETIC DEPT.

their own 3-yard line. Scott had to kick from the end zone, so he stood back as far as he could. He punched the pigskin with all his might.

The ball sailed high in the air—right into the teeth of a 50-mph gale. Iowa punt returner Leo Dick was waiting for the ball on the Indiana 25-yard line. He noticed that the ball seemed to hang in the air over the 20-yard line. So he trotted in a few steps. But because of the stiff wind, the ball began drifting backward. Dick trotted in a few more steps. But he was not much closer to the ball. It was now descending, and sailing steadily backward.

Dick broke into a wild dash and finally caught the ball—right in the Indiana end zone—for a touchdown!

SEAN LANDETA

Punter ■ New York Giants ■ Jan. 5, 1986

It's one thing to swing at a baseball or even a golf ball and miss. But how does a punter miss a football? Ask Sean Landeta. He's responsible for the most disgraceful punt in NFL play-off history.

The New York Giants and Chicago Bears were playing in the Windy City. Midway through the first quarter, Landeta was sent in to punt from his own goal line.

Landeta took the snap as the Bears launched an all-out rush. He released the ball to kick, and he swung his leg. Incredibly, he missed the ball! The pigskin barely touched his instep, skipping off to his right.

It dropped to the turf, where Chicago defender Shaun Gayle scooped it up at the 5-yard line. Gayle scampered into the end zone for the first touchdown of the game. Landeta's blunder went down as a minus-7-yard punt. It should have been listed as an attempted punt.

Landeta felt like climbing into a hole—the 7–0 hole he had dug for his Giants. New York went on to lose 21–0.

"I couldn't believe it," he said. "It's something that never happened to me before. I mean, you don't even miss a ball just fooling around."

He claimed the wind gusted just as he started to punt, making the ball do tricks. Isn't it strange? In all the years of pro football, the wind waited to do that until this pressure-packed game. Maybe the wind knew it would be on TV when it made the first player ever strike out on a punt.

Landeta had suffered another moment like that three weeks earlier in another big game. This time, the Giants were playing the Dallas Cowboys. Landeta was set to punt deep inside his 5-yard line. He couldn't get his punt off because of a fierce Cowboy rush. So he tried his version of a forward pass. He underhanded the ball right into the back of a teammate, setting up the winning touchdown for Dallas.

EVERY TRICK
IN THE BOOK

If good sportsmanship were a requirement, some teams would have to forfeit. That's because they make an end run around the rule book. It's part of their game plan. They are so unfair they don't even know how to call for a fair catch. For the "The Sneakiest Trickery Ever Pulled," The Football Hall of SHAME inducts the following:

GEORGIA BULLDOGS

Oct. 26, 1912

Georgia's Bulldogs pulled the denim over the Alabama Crimson Tide's eyes—with a pair of coveralls.

In the first play of the game, Georgia lined up on its own 20-yard line. Only ten Bulldogs were in formation, but Alabama failed to notice. The eleventh, flanker Alonzo Awtrey, stood just inside the 15-yard sideline. He was dressed in white overalls and was holding a water bucket.

The Tide didn't pay him any attention because they thought he was the waterboy.

When the ball was snapped, Awtrey dropped his bucket and sped upfield. Quarterback Timon Bowden fired a pass to Awtrey. He made it to the 50 before he was finally tackled by a befuddled defender.

Once the Alabama fans realized what had happened, they rushed onto the field to protest. They were met by the fired-up Georgia crowd, and a brawl started. The local police broke it up, taking dozens of Dawgs and Tidesmen to jail.

Meanwhile, an Alabama official tracked down Georgia's acting athletic director, John Morris. He demanded in the name of sportsmanship that Morris call the play back. When Morris refused, the official flattened him—presumably in the name of sportsmanship.

Georgia's coach, W. A. Cunningham, who dreamed up the sneaky play, began to feel a little guilty and humble. He offered to forget the whole matter and start the game over at the original line of scrimmage. But the officials said there was no rule at the time against what the Bulldogs had done. They allowed the play to stand.

The Bulldogs went on to win 13–9.

At its next meeting, the collegiate rules committee closed the loophole, forcing Georgia to hang up its coveralls for good.

NOTRE DAME "FAINTING IRISH"

Nov. 21, 1953

Unbeaten Notre Dame avoided a major upset by the Iowa Hawkeyes with a fraud that worked to perfection not once, but twice.

The Hawkeyes fought hard and held a surprising 7–0 lead late in the second quarter. The heavily favored Fighting Irish put together a long drive down to Iowa's 12-yard line. But they were out of time-outs and only a few seconds remained in the half. Notre Dame appeared to be beaten by the clock.

Suddenly, tackle Frank Varrichione flopped to the ground in a dead faint. The referee called an official's time-out, stopping the clock with just two seconds left. The injured player was carted off the field.

Varrichione was faking. The only real hurt he suffered was the thought that underdog Iowa was winning. His act was a designed play. It was used in emergencies when the team needed to stop the clock. Notre Dame coach Frank Leahy even had Varrichione run the fake injury in practice.

The first time he rehearsed it, Varrichione acted in true Hollywood fashion. He clutched his leg, moaned, screamed, and collapsed. But Leahy thought it had been a bit overdone. "Frank," said Leahy, "I think we'd better make it total unconsciousness."

That's exactly how Varrichione played it in the Iowa game. His fake injury gave Notre Dame time to pull off one more play—a 9-yard touchdown pass. The half ended in a 7–7 tie.

In the final seconds of the game, the Fighting Irish used the phony injury play again.

Notre Dame had used up its time-outs in a last-ditch drive. Stalled at the Iowa 10-yard line, they trailed 14–7 as the clock ticked toward zero.

Suddenly, both Irish captain Don Penza and tackle Art Hunter fell to the ground—seemingly unconscious. (Actually, three other players also hit the turf at the same time. One of them was Varrichione, who made an amazing halftime recovery from his "injury." But quarterback Ralph Guglielmi kicked them in the rear and ordered them to get up. No one would fall for the idea of five injured Fighting Irish.)

But the refs bought the two-man act starring Penza and Hunter. With time to regroup thanks to the official time-out, Guglielmi tossed a touchdown pass. Just six seconds were left in the game. The point-after kick tied the game—a game that started a storm of protest.

The NCAA declared the phony-injury play "dishonest, unsportsmanlike, and contrary to the rules." Then it handed down new rules to forbid faking injuries to stop the clock.

The fraud tarnished Notre Dame's image. In fact, Leahy's boys were called the "Fainting Irish." They were further stung by the college football ratings. Because of the tainted tie, Notre Dame tumbled from the top of the heap to No. 2. They remained there for the rest of the season, even though their unbeaten record was better than that of No. 1 Maryland.

All this provided little comfort to the Iowa fans, though. All they could do was scream bloody murder over getting cheated out of a victory.

Iowa coach Forest Evashevski borrowed a few lines from the great sportswriter Grantland Rice. He told fans: "When that one great scorer comes to write against your name/He writes not that you won or lost/ But how come we got gypped at Notre Dame???"

IOWA HAWKEYES

Nov. 8, 1914

With the game all but won, the Iowa Hawkeyes set out to disgrace the Northwestern Wildcats. How? By playing them for suckers with a sneaky scam—the old penalty trick.

During the first half of the game (won by Iowa 27–0), Hawkeye quarterback Sammy Gross kept complaining to officials. Time and again he accused Northwestern's defensive line of fouls. The irritated Wildcats told Gross to shut up and called him a crybaby.

That's exactly how Gross wanted his opponents to react. He was setting them up for his flimflam.

Late in the fourth quarter, Iowa was on its own 16-yard line. Gross brought his team up to the line of scrimmage. Then he turned to the referee and asked that a penalty be called. He wanted the opposing defensive left end charged with holding on the previous play.

The innocent end denied any guilt. The ref, losing patience with the whining Gross, shouted, "Play ball!"

Gross walked up to his center, Max Houghton. In a voice loud enough for the opposing team to hear, Gross said, "Give me the ball. I'll walk off the penalty myself."

Houghton shook his head and said, "You can't get away with that, Sammy. It's your own funeral, and you'll be kicked out of the game." But the center snapped the ball back to Gross anyway. That put the ball in play.

As the Northwestern defenders stood watching, Gross walked past the line of scrimmage with the pigskin under his arm. He started pacing off the penalty toward the Wildcats' goal. He shoved Northwestern's defensive back Rollin Gray aside, saying, "Get out of my way."

"Goodbye, Sammy. They'll throw you out of the game for that!" shouted Gray, not realizing the ball was in play. Gross took several more steps and then broke for the open field. He ran 54 yards before Gray brought him down.

Iowa had pulled off the same play a year earlier against Nebraska. The only difference was that Gross had run only 15 yards before he was tackled—by the referee, who smelled something fishy and put a stop to the phony penalty trick.

CARLISLE INDUSTRIAL SCHOOL INDIANS

Oct. 31, 1903

The crafty Carlisle Indians loved nothing better than winning through trickery. Their greatest trick play ever, though, was outsmarting the whiz kids from Harvard.

At first, it looked like it was Harvard that had outwitted Carlisle.

The week before the Harvard game, Carlisle played Syracuse. Indians coach Pop Warner ran one of his many scams. Every time the Carlisle center snapped the ball, every player in the backfield seemed to be running with it. Warner had patches shaped like footballs sewn on every player's jersey!

A Harvard alumnus happened to be at the Syracuse game. He warned Crimson coach Percy Haughton to be on the lookout for the scheme. When the Indians arrived for their game against Harvard, Haughton asked Warner to remove the patches. But Warner said there was nothing in the rules outlawing them.

Haughton then directed his manager to bring out the footballs to be used in the game. To Warner's surprise, every ball had been painted crimson—the color of Harvard's jerseys. "You can't do that!" complained Warner. Haughton just smiled and said, "There's nothing in the rules outlawing them." So both coaches agreed to use regulation balls, and the patches were removed from the Indians' jerseys.

Although Warner was foiled, he still had one trick left up his sleeve. He waited until the start of the second half to spring it on Harvard. Then he ordered his team to use the "hidden ball" or "hunchback" play.

The kickoff was fielded by quarterback Jimmie Johnson on the 5-yard line. Instead of blocking for him, the rest of the Indians gathered around Johnson. Using this huddle as a shield, Johnson slipped the ball up the back of guard Charlie Dillon's jersey. Dillon had an elastic band around the bottom of his jersey to keep the ball from falling out.

Once the ball was safely tucked away, Johnson yelled "Go!" The Indians fanned out in a long line across the field. They bounded like deer toward the Harvard goal. Each back yanked off his leather helmet, hugging it to his chest and pretending it was the football, to fake out the Harvard players even more.

The Indian backs were chased and slammed to the ground. When their tacklers found only headgear, and no football, they began jumping around, trying to find the ball carrier.

Dillon, Carlisle's six-foot guard, was running with both arms free. But none of the Crimson paid any attention to him. Posing as a blocker, Dillon headed straight for Harvard's last defender, safety Carl Marshall. Marshall sidestepped him, thinking Dillon was attempting to block. Then Marshall dashed up the field to join his teammates in a frantic search for the football.

Meanwhile, the fans in the grandstands could see the lump under Dillon's jersey. Their puzzled buzz turned into a roar of laughter. They pointed at the strange hump on Dillon's back.

But the Harvard players were still scurrying around as Dillon loped across the goal line. He pulled the ball out from under his jersey, placed it on the ground, and sat on it. On the bench, Pop Warner giggled with glee.

Unfortunately for Carlisle's tricksters, the Crimson had the last laugh. Harvard beat Carlisle 21–11.

RON MEYER

Coach ■ New England Patriots ■ Dec. 12, 1982

Patriots coach Ron Meyer really "snowed" the Miami Dolphins, and broke the ice in a scoreless tie.

The Dolphins and Patriots were playing in a blinding

blizzard in Foxboro, Massachusetts, in 1982. Because of the snowstorm, neither team had even come close to making a touchdown. To boot, each failed at a field goal attempt because of the bad weather.

However, with 4:45 remaining, New England engineered a decent drive. But they stalled out at the Miami 16-yard line. The Patriots then called time so kicker John Smith could clear away a spot on the snow-covered field. It was a crucial field goal attempt that could win the game.

Suddenly, a light went on in Coach Meyer's mind. "I saw John Smith on his hands and knees trying to get the snow cleared, and all of a sudden it hit me," recalled Meyer. "Why not send a snowplow out there?"

Meyer raced down the sideline to Mark Henderson. He operated the snowplow that had been clearing the yard lines during time-outs. Meyer told Henderson to make a spot on the field for Smith.

With the snowplow, Henderson retraced his path along the 20-yard line. Then, catching officials and Dolphins off guard, he swept snow ahead of him. He left a perfect patch of green SuperTurf between the 23- and 25-yard lines. It was the best sweep the Patriots fans had seen in years.

"I saw him coming," said Miami defensive tackle Bob Baumhower. "But what was I supposed to do? No way I'm going to take on a plow."

When play resumed, Smith planted his foot squarely in the place cleared by Henderson. He kicked a game-winning 33-yard field goal to give the Patriots a 3–0 victory.

CORNELL BIG RED

Oct. 9, 1965

To defend against a field goal kicker, the Cornell Big Red literally rose to the occasion—and stooped to a new low.

Their opponents were the Princeton Tigers. They had marched to the Big Red 19-yard line before their

Cornell defense stands head and shoulders above the rest.
ROBERT P. MATTHEWS

36

drive sputtered early in the game. Charlie Gogolak, Princeton's soccer-style kicker, trotted onto the gridiron to attempt a field goal.

As the Tigers broke their huddle and lined up for the kick, they couldn't believe their eyes. Cornell had built two human towers. Defensive backs Jim Docherty and Dale Witwer had climbed onto the shoulders of six-foot five-inch tackles Reeve Vanneman and Harry Garman.

"I thought they were just joking around," Gogolak said later. "It was like a bad dream. I would have liked to hit one of those guys in the head. I'll bet they were up there praying they wouldn't be hit."

As he got ready for the snap, Gogolak noticed that the towers were not lined up evenly with the goal posts. He figured that by aiming his kick slightly to the left, he could still make the score.

Unfortunately for Gogolak, he aimed the ball a little too far to the left. He missed the field goal. Unfortunately for Cornell, it didn't matter. The Big Red was penalized 5 yards for being offside. The penalty gave the Tigers a first down, allowing them to complete the touchdown drive.

The tower scheme crumbled after Gogolak booted field goals of 44 and 54 yards over the stacked defense. Princeton won 36–27.

After that season, The Rules Committee condemned the twin towers.

TACKLING DUMMIES

There's nothing like a clean, crisp tackle that drives a ball carrier into the ground. Fans "ooh" and "aah" over the clothesline tackle, the gang tackle, and the shoulder tackle. But they also boo and jeer the player who makes a stupid tackle that goes against the grain of decent football. For "The Tackiest Tackles Ever Made," The Football Hall of SHAME inducts the following:

LARRY "THE WILD MAN" EISENHAUER

Defensive End ■ Boston Patriots ■ Sept. 1961

The cruelest tackle ever seen on TV was made by Larry "The Wild Man" Eisenhauer.

It was captured on film and shown on a popular kiddie show, of all places. The show was "Boom Town," and it starred Rex Trailer and his comic side-kick, Pablo the clown.

The producers thought it would be funny if Pablo—a

skinny, middle-aged shrimp—tried out for the Patriots. The team agreed to go along with the gag. Pablo dressed up in an old-fashioned football uniform and joined the Patriots on the practice field.

The script called for a mock scrimmage. Pablo would get the handoff and zigzag his way through the Patriot defense for a touchdown. The producers knew the kids at home would love it. They'd laugh at seeing professional football players running around and falling down as Pablo scampered past them.

The script was good, but the TV people had overlooked one important factor—Eisenhauer. He wasn't called "The Wild Man" for nothing. He would get so psyched up before a game that he would punch anything, walls, doors, lockers—even teammates weren't safe. He once put his helmeted head through a locker-room wall in Buffalo. Another time, in Kansas City, he worked himself into a real frenzy. He got so excited that he charged out onto the field, forgetting he was wearing nothing but his helmet.

Unfortunately, the director of the show didn't know about "The Wild Man." So he didn't know about his fierce dedication to football. As the cameras rolled, Pablo began snaking his way through the Patriot defense. Everything was going smoothly until Pablo scooted down to the 20-yard line past the last defender. It just happened to be Eisenhauer.

Suddenly, the six-foot five-inch, 255-pound Patriot was overcome by his killer instinct. All he saw was an enemy player running for a touchdown. And he had to stop the enemy. Eisenhauer let out a terrifying roar and charged after the five-foot three-inch, 110-pound clown.

Poor Pablo. With eyes as big as footballs, Pablo ran

for his life, but it was no contest. At about the 5-yard line, Eisenhauer jumped on his back and squashed him. Boomed Eisenhauer, "Nobody gets across our goal line! Not even a clown!"

Pablo was buried in the turf, gasping for breath. The TV crew rushed to his aid. Then they turned and chastised Eisenhauer.

"I'm kind of ashamed of it now," he said recently. "But I just couldn't stand to see anybody score on us if there was a chance I could stop him. He was slow, so it wasn't any trick catching him. I didn't really hurt him. I just sort of jumped on his back. Why give a guy a free touchdown?"

J. V. KING

Reporter ■ Oct. 18, 1897

Reporter J. V. King tackled his assignment with too much gusto. In covering the game between Colgate's Red Raiders and the Syracuse Orangemen, he didn't just report the story, he *was* the story.

King could hardly be called an objective reporter. The previous year he had starred on Colgate's football team. He had even scored the winning touchdown against Syracuse. After graduation, he joined the staff of a newspaper in Hamilton, New York—home of his alma mater.

Now, as a cub reporter, he was sent to cover Colgate's home game against Syracuse. King watched the two teams battle, taking notes from the sidelines. Actually, he did more than just watch and take notes.

Early in the second half of a tie game, Syracuse ball carrier Haden Patten broke into the clear. He was headed for a touchdown. Being a man of noble impulse, King decided to save his alma mater. With notepad in one hand and pencil in the other, he rushed onto the field. Then, without even removing his hat, he tackled Patten.

Players, officials, and spectators argued over what should be done. The play was upheld, and the game ended in a 6–6 tie. Syracuse vowed to get even. They refused to play Colgate—in any sport—for the next five years.

Meanwhile, King's outrageous tackle made big news. One local newspaper wrote, "Colgate should get him back in college and on the team, where he can make his tackles within the rules of the game and save his good clothes and hat."

BOBBY YANDELL

Halfback ■ Mississippi Rebels ■ Nov. 29, 1941

No tackle was tackier than the one made by Bobby Yandell. He brought down his own teammate!

It couldn't have come at a worse time. The Ole Miss Rebels were battling their arch rivals, the Mississippi State Bulldogs. The prize at stake was the Southeastern Conference championship. In the second quarter, the score was tied at 0–0. The Rebels had the ball on their own 45-yard line. Tailback Junior Hovious dropped back to throw a pass—either to Yandell or to end Ray Poole.

Bobby Yandell tackled his own man.
AP/WIDE WORLD PHOTOS

With a neat move, Poole broke free and had his defender beat by a few steps. But the backfield was crowded with onrushing linemen. Hovious was scrambling for his life. Poole saw that Hovious was in trouble. He put on the brakes and doubled back just as the ball was thrown.

Poole's defender had the bead on the interception. But Poole managed to jump high enough to snare the ball. Meanwhile, Yandell, who was right in front of the play, somehow got himself turned around. In the process, he became totally confused about who was running where.

Poole twisted free from the grasp of the defender. He had an open field ahead of him. It looked like a sure touchdown. Nobody could stop him now. Nobody but his own teammate. Poole started to take off for the goal line, expecting Yandell to block for him. Instead, in his fuzzy state of mind, Yandell tackled him at the Bulldog 46-yard line.

Yandell had killed the Rebels' big chance to score. Unable to overcome his blunder, Ole Miss failed to keep the drive alive.

The boneheaded tackle proved costly. Without the "sure touchdown," the Rebels lost the game 6–0 and the SEC title.

TOMMY LEWIS

Fullback ■ Alabama Crimson Tide ■ Jan. 1, 1954

With one tackle, Tommy Lewis secured his place in the history of football—and of shame.

What he did caused an uproar in the Cotton Bowl. He leaped off the bench and tackled a touchdown-bound runner. Lewis was too competitive and too emotional for his own good.

It happened midway into the second period, with the Rice Owls leading Alabama, 7–6. The Owls recovered a fumble by Crimson Tide quarterback Bart Starr on their own 5-yard line. On the next play, the Owls sprang halfback Dick Moegle, who skirted right end. With clear sailing ahead, he dashed upfield along the sideline.

Lewis, who had been elected team captain for the game, watched in horror from the bench. "He's going all the way!" he shouted in alarm. When Moegle reached the 48-yard line, he was directly in front of Lewis. The super-competitive 'Bama back could no longer control himself. Lewis gave in to the urge that has tempted football players for decades.

Acting on pure impulse, Lewis charged onto the field. He didn't even have his helmet on. At the 44-yard line, he tackled Moegle, who tumbled to the 38-yard line. Then Lewis moved sheepishly back to his spot on the sideline. He plopped down on the bench. As the startled crowd gasped, he buried his head in his hands.

Immediately after the shocking tackle, the officials awarded Moegle a touchdown. He was given credit for a 95-yard run. There was no protest from the Alabama bench.

Moegle put on a dazzling show throughout the game. He racked up 264 yards and led Rice to a 28–6 victory. But it was Lewis who stole the limelight.

"I'm too emotional," he told reporters after the game. "I kept telling myself, 'I didn't do it. I didn't do it.' But I knew I had." Lewis went to the Rice dressing room at halftime to apologize. He told the press, "I'm just too full of Alabama."

Strangely, the public didn't cast any blame on Lewis. People hailed him as a "great competitor." He was buried under a mound of sympathetic letters. Telegrams and offers to appear on radio and TV shows and to speak at banquets poured in. Lewis even appeared on "The Ed Sullivan Show," where he received a thunderous ovation.

The public shouldn't have been so kind. Lewis' off-the-bench tackle hurt Alabama more than fans realized. Films show that Moegle would have been tackled a few yards downfield anyway. The Tide's speedy back, Bill Oliver, was in good position for a clear shot at Moegle. If Lewis hadn't interfered, Oliver could have shoved Moegle out of bounds at the 35-yard line—just three yards from where Lewis beat him to it.

The touchdown awarded to Rice did more than give the Owls a 14–6 lead. It changed the momentum—and then the outcome—of the game.

SNOOZE PLAYS

Coaches and players memorize every detail of the game plan and the playbook. Baloney! These guys daydream and forget things just like other students do. The only problem is that their classroom is the playing field. When they get caught napping, they're in for a rude awakening. For "The Most Mind-Boggling Mental Miscues," The Football Hall of SHAME inducts the following:

FRANCIS SCHMIDT

Coach ■ Tulsa–Arkansas–Texas Christian–Ohio State–Idaho ■ 1919–42

No coach was more absentminded than Francis Schmidt.

His head was locked into football twenty-four hours a day, seven days a week. He didn't just daydream about the game. He weekdreamed it. Every cell in his brain was filled with little X's and O's.

Schmidt was even more absorbed with football than

Howard Jones, his forgetful peer. Jones was coach of the University of Southern California from 1925–40. His mind was centered so deeply on the game that he ignored traffic signals. He also misplaced keys and missed appointments. He even got lost on his way home. But even Jones couldn't top Schmidt for being forgetful.

Schmidt would stamp a letter and sit on it to be sure the stamp stuck. Then he would forget where the letter was. Raging, he would scatter the papers on his desk in a pointless search. Finally someone would get the nerve to tell him he was sitting on it. "Well," Schmidt would growl, "why didn't you tell me sooner?"

Schmidt's memory gaps caused him much pain on the sidelines. In 1927, when he was at Arkansas, carpenters built a shelter over the Razorback bench. They finished it just before a game against Oklahoma State. During the game, a pass went through the arms of an Arkansas defender. It ended up in the hands of an Oklahoma State receiver for a touchdown. Schmidt was so upset he leaped off the bench. Forgetting about the new shelter, he struck his head against it and knocked himself out cold.

He wiped himself out again in a tense game in 1931. This time, he was coaching at Texas Christian. Enraged by a penalty against his team, Schmidt charged onto the field. There was just one problem. He hadn't removed the headphones he used to talk with his assistant in the press box. When Schmidt reached the end of the wire, it flipped him over.

A few years later, Schmidt became head coach at Ohio State. He and an assistant left on a recruiting trip. When they stopped for gas, the assistant went into the cafe next door. Schmidt stayed in the car, making notes. Once the tank was filled and he had paid for the gas, Schmidt drove off. He totally forgot about the assistant he was leaving behind.

Schmidt once took his car to a gas station in Columbus for an oil change. While the car was up on the rack, he stayed behind the wheel drawing plays in a notebook. Mindless of the world around him, the coach pored over his diagrams. In a few minutes, he came up with a play that looked unstoppable. With a cry of triumph, he slapped the notebook shut, opened the door, stepped out—and fell ten feet to the concrete below.

HERBERT HOOVER

Manager ■ Stanford Cardinals ■ March 19, 1892

Herbert Hoover, who later became President of the United States, organized Stanford's football team. He also set up its first big game, against arch rival California. But the game almost didn't happen, because he forgot one minor detail—the football!

As team manager, Hoover had 15,000 tickets printed up for the contest. The game drew such a huge crowd that Hoover ran out of tickets by early afternoon. At the gate, he was forced to collect coins any way he could. He put them in empty washtubs, boxes, and anything else he could scrounge up.

As the 3 P.M. kickoff time approached, the 20,000 banner-waving, shouting fans tingled with excitement. It was the start of what would become a long and fierce football rivalry.

Both teams were pumped up and eager for action. They roared their approval when referee Jack Sherrard signaled them to get ready. Then the ref asked Hoover for the game ball.

Hoover's jaw dropped. He thought he had taken care of everything. He had arranged for the tickets, the stadium, the concessions, and the security. But he plum forgot to bring a football!

While the crowd moaned and fidgeted, a man named David Goulcher hopped on his horse and galloped into town for a ball. He owned a sporting goods store in downtown San Francisco. He returned an hour later, a hero. But the players' cheers quickly turned to groans. Goulcher hadn't brought a regulation football.

Instead, the teams had to play the delayed game (won by Stanford 14–10) with an inflated bladder.

ED JONTOS

Coach ■ Rensselaer Poly Institute Engineers ■ Oct. 4, 1947

Coach Ed Jontos could have kicked himself for losing a game that seemed like a shoo-in for his Engineers.

Rensselaer Poly was leading the University of Buffalo 7–0 in the third quarter. Jontos' star player, defensive end Stan Gorzelnic, came to the sidelines. He pointed to his left shoe, which was badly ripped.

Because the football program had a tight budget, the team didn't have any spare shoes. So Jontos did the next best thing. He searched up and down the bench for a replacement shoe. But Gorzelnic had big feet. Really big feet.

"Who wears a size 13?" Jontos asked his bench-warmers. No one said a word. "Take off your shoes," he barked. "You don't know what size you're wearing anyway."

Jontos checked one shoe after another, but it was no use. There wasn't a size 13 among them. Meanwhile, without Gorzelnic on defense, Buffalo scored two touchdowns. They ran the ball right at—and through—his substitute.

Jontos was beside himself with anger. Eventually, the team trainer performed a crude repair job on the battered shoe. But Gorzelnic returned to the game too late. The Engineers lost 14–7.

In the losers' locker room, the players were glum. As they were undressing in silence, Jontos shouted, "We lost the game because of a shoe!" Then he yanked off one of his shoes and flung it, just missing a lineman. The player picked up the shoe and casually glanced inside. It was none other than a size 13.

ROY "WRONG WAY" RIEGELS

Center ■ California Golden Bears ■ Jan. 1, 1929

Roy Riegels carved his name in college football history as the all-time No. 1 bonehead.

He forgot which way to run!

Riegels not only cost his school a Rose Bowl victory, he also became a legend among bumblers and earned a

Roy Riegels discovers he ran the wrong way.
AP/WIDE WORLD PHOTOS

new nickname—"Wrong Way." And he did it all in about ten seconds.

It all began in the second quarter of Pasadena's annual big game. The California Golden Bears and the Georgia Tech Yellow Jackets were locked in a scoreless tie.

Tech running back Stumpy Thomason was hit on his own 36-yard line and fumbled. The ball bounced to the Tech 40 with both teams in hot pursuit. There was a wild scramble for the loose ball. Riegels, the California center, picked it out of the air. He started running

51

downfield in the right direction. But only 30 yards away from a go-ahead touchdown, his radar went haywire. Pivoting to get away from a tackler, Riegels completely lost his bearings. He wheeled around in a U-turn and legged it out for all he was worth toward his own end zone.

Centers aren't supposed to be fast runners. But Riegels was sprinting like a man possessed. He was pumped up with the stuff of which heroes are made. Some of his teammates were fooled by his misguided attempt at glory. They began knocking down Georgia Tech tacklers, who seemed confused themselves.

The legendary sports broadcaster Graham McNamee was calling the play-by-play on radio. He couldn't believe his eyes. "What's the matter with me?" he shouted into the microphone. "Am I going crazy?"

The Tech players on the bench jumped up and began to shout. But coach Bill Alexander ordered them to sit down. "He's running the wrong way," the coach said. "Let's see how far he can go."

If it hadn't been for Benny Lom, the California quarterback, Riegels would have gone all the way. Lom immediately chased his teammate, shouting, "Stop, Roy! You're going the wrong way!" At the 10-yard line, Lom caught Riegels and slowed him down with a bear hug. But Riegels shook him off. "Get away from me!" shrieked Riegels. "This is my touchdown!" At the 3-yard line, Lom grabbed him again. This time the quarterback held on. Riegels finally realized something was wrong, and turned around. Just then a wave of Georgia Tech players smeared him on the one-yard line.

Riegels had run nearly 70 yards in the wrong direction! He sat on the ground in shock. His teammates came over to console him. They had always looked up to him. In fact, before the game, they had voted him captain for the next season.

California decided the best way out of the jam was to punt. But Lom's kick from the end zone was blocked for a safety. It turned out to be the key play of the game. The safety gave the Yellow Jackets the two points they needed for an 8–7 victory.

After the safety, the dejected Riegels took himself out of the game. But after his teammates insisted, he played the entire second half.

In time, the Rules Committee adopted a new rule on fumbles. It forbids an opponent from advancing a fumble that strikes the ground. But the rule change couldn't erase the shame of Riegels' wrong-way run.

NEW YORK JETS

Jan. 13, 1969

Every pro football team strives for one goal—winning the Super Bowl. Nothing is more important than bringing home that dazzling trophy. A priceless, sought-after symbol, it proves that a team is the best in the world.

The cocky, upstart New York Jets, led by Broadway Joe Namath, coveted that trophy. From the start of the 1968 season, they made it plain that they wanted it. And they were determined to win it.

At Super Bowl III in Miami, the Jets represented the American Football League. They were 18-point underdogs against the National Football League's Baltimore

Colts. But Namath had his heart set on capturing the trophy. He boldly declared, "The Jets will win on Sunday. I guarantee it."

Namath was true to his word. In a stunning upset that shocked the sports world, the Jets whomped the Colts 16–7. They had won the Super Bowl.

The grand prize was theirs, in all its gleaming glory. The 21-inch sterling-silver championship trophy signified that the Jets were No. 1. Just wait, said the team, until the fans back in New York see this. Unfortunately for the fans, that's exactly what they had to do: wait.

When the Jets flew home from Miami, they forgot the very thing they had worked so hard to get—the trophy!

"That wasn't exactly our finest hour, especially coming right after our finest game," admitted Frank Ramos, the Jets' public relations director.

"On the flight back to New York, it was one of those 'Who's got the trophy?' 'Do you have the trophy?' 'Where is the trophy?'

"When we got back home, a big crowd was waiting. It sure was embarrassing when all those fans asked to see the trophy we'd won and we didn't have anything to show them."

So where was the trophy? An assistant found it back at the team's Fort Lauderdale hotel, next to a bunch of left-behind equipment.

RED FRIESELL

Nov. 16, 1940

In one of the dumbest official blunders ever, referee Red Friesell allowed Cornell to score a winning TD—on fifth down.

Friesell showed what a poor math student he was during a game in Hanover, New Hampshire. Cornell's opponent was the Dartmouth Big Green. Rated No. 1 in the nation, Cornell was riding an 18-game winning streak. Dartmouth was a two-touchdown underdog.

Dartmouth amazed the experts and played inspired football. With only a minute to play, the Big Green held a slim 3–0 lead. Then Cornell drove down to the Dartmouth 6-yard line. The Dartmouth defense stiffened. Cornell failed to score on three runs and an incomplete pass.

The Big Green fans and players jumped for joy. Only three seconds remained, and it was Dartmouth's ball. Or was it? Counting like a preschooler, Friesell signaled a fourth down for Cornell on the Dartmouth 6-yard line. Dartmouth's protests fell on deaf ears. None of the three other officials questioned Friesell's boneheaded ruling.

Given a surprise gift, Cornell lined up for an unheard of fifth down. On the final play, quarterback Walt Scholl lofted a pass to halfback Bill Murphy. It was caught in the end zone for a dramatic, but dishonest, 7–3 victory.

All night long, the town of Hanover fumed. Dummy figures of the officials were burned. Films of the game proved beyond any doubt that Friesell had made a mistake.

Cornell had won illegally. But to its credit, the school gave up the victory three days later. They declared that Dartmouth had won the game 3–0.

Friesell's foul-up made headlines across America, and he heard from coaches everywhere. Ohio State's Francis Schmidt, whose team was trounced by Michigan 40–0, wired Friesell: "WISH YOU HAD WORKED OUR GAME SATURDAY. WE NEEDED SOMETHING." Dicky Pond, coach of Yale, which was drubbed 28–0 by Harvard that same afternoon, telegrammed the referee: "ENTIRE STUDENT BODY BREATHLESSLY AWAITING WORD FROM YOU REGARDING HARVARD GAME. DID WE REALLY LOSE? CAN'T YOU DO SOMETHING FOR US?"

Friesell had been scoffed at enough and needed a little sympathy. So what did conference commissioner Asa Bushnell do? He wired the beleaguered official: "DON'T LET IT GET YOU DOWN, DOWN, DOWN, DOWN, DOWN."

POOP TALKS

*Pep talks are designed by coaches to inspire
teams and give players the desire to go beyond their limits. Too often, though, the
coaches are the ones who exceed the limits—of good taste, behavior, and emotion.
There should be a penalty for illegal use of
the tongue. For "The Zaniest Pep Talks Ever
Delivered," The Football Hall of SHAME
inducts the following:*

DAN DEVINE

Coach ■ Missouri Tigers ■ Nov. 18, 1967

No matter how well plays are designed, they don't
always work out the way the coach plans. Dan Devine
found the same was true with pep talks.

To rev up his Tigers for a game against Nebraska,
Devine decided to make his team sick of the Corn-
huskers' fight song.

In 1966, Nebraska whipped Missouri 35–0. Every
time the Huskers scored, the band played "There Is No

Place Like Nebraska." The band sat right behind the Missouri bench, so the Tigers got an earful of the song.

Devine hated the song. He figured hearing it would fire his team up and spur them on to victory in 1967. So he ordered the team manager to play only that record all week before the game. Every day as they changed, showered, and dressed, all the Tigers heard was the Nebraska fight song.

By game day, Devine had his players primed for a special pep talk. It was sure to motivate them. "I never want to hear that song again!" he thundered. Then he grabbed the record and flung it to the locker-room floor.

Devine had expected the disk to break into a hundred pieces on the cement floor. The idea was to make a visual impact on the players before they charged onto the field.

But things didn't go according to plan. To his dismay, the record didn't break. Instead, it bounced straight up and hit the ceiling.

That was Devine's first clue that his scheme was in danger of failing. He picked up the record and slammed it to the floor a second time. But, once again, it survived. Clenching his teeth, he tried to snap the record in half. The record bent, but it didn't break. Frustrated and red-faced with anger, Devine hurled the record against the wall. It bounced back like a tennis ball.

"I don't know when I've ever been so embarrassed and humiliated," Devine recalled. "Finally, I just went over to a window, opened it, and threw the record out. Then I got out of there as fast as I could."

Despite their coach's terrible performance, the Tigers won 10–7.

KNUTE ROCKNE

Coach ■ Notre Dame Fighting Irish ■ Oct. 28, 1922

Knute Rockne would do anything to psyche up his team before a big game. He'd even lie through his teeth.

Playing Georgia Tech in Atlanta, Rockne felt his underdog team needed extra inspiration. The Yellow Jackets had been undefeated at home for several years.

In the locker room, he showed the players telegrams from important alumni. Then he told his team, "I have one wire here, boys, that probably doesn't mean much to you, but it does to me." He took a deep breath and his voice began to crack. "It's from my poor sick little boy Billy, who is critically ill in the hospital."

Rockne's throat tightened. His lips trembled and his eyes watered as he read Billy's touching wire: "I want Daddy's team to win."

The players were touched by this tear-jerking request from the coach's ailing son. They roared out of the locker room and ripped Georgia Tech apart 13–3.

A cheering crowd of 20,000 greeted the victorious Irish at the train station in South Bend, Indiana. And who was skipping about in front of all the other well-wishers? None other than "sick" little Billy Rockne—in picture-perfect health. Of course, Billy hadn't been ill at all. Rockne had sent the fake telegram himself.

That wasn't the only time Rockne used a cock-and-bull story. Before the November 16, 1929 game against the University of Southern California, Rockne told

Knute Rockne psyches up his players during practice.
NOTRE DAME SPORTS INFORMATION DEPT.

alumnus Joe Byrne, "We're going to lose today. The team has been lethargic all week. The only way to win is if I can think of something that would give the boys an emotional lift."

In the locker room, Rockne told his team, "Boys, I'm getting this pressure from the alumni. My wife Bonnie can't take it any longer, and my children are being ridiculed at school. I am resigning. Please let me go out a winner. Go out there and win, WIN!"

Notre Dame beat USC 13–12. Afterward, Byrne

asked Rockne, "What are you going to tell the boys when you see them at practice next Monday?"

"What do you mean, what will I tell them? I *am* resigning—unless I get a letter of apology from the alumni."

Rockne had told such a good fib that he had even convinced himself it was true!

GRANT TEAFF

Coach ■ Baylor Bears ■ Nov. 25, 1978

In what may be the grossest pre-game talk ever given, Grant Teaff made his Baylor Bears watch him eat a worm.

What this had to do with football was anybody's guess. However, the Bears did charge out of the locker room with such force that they broke the hinges off the door. That was no surprise. They all wanted to throw up.

Teaff bit off more than he could chew. The Bears had been preparing for a game against the highly favored Texas Longhorns. Baylor was going into the contest with an awful 2–8 record and several key players injured. Teaff decided that his team needed to stay loose.

During a team meeting, Teaff had told a joke about two Eskimos fishing through the ice. One was catching fish and the other wasn't. The unsuccessful angler asked his partner what his secret was. The successful fisherman opened his mouth and pulled out a slimy worm. He replied, "You've got to keep the worms warm."

Grant Teaff hopes he won't ever have to eat another worm.
AP/WIDE WORLD PHOTOS

The tale gave Teaff a nauseating idea. On the day of the game, he bought a box of worms. He cleaned one of them and put it in his pocket. Moments before game time, he told his players, "The game is yours, but there's one thing I'll do for you. I'll keep the worms warm." Then he took the worm out, dropped it in his mouth, and ate it.

Strangely, the Bears were inspired by Teaff's revolting pep talk. They destroyed mighty Texas 38–14.

Later, one of the players approached the coach and said, "I noticed you turned a bright shade of purple after eating the worm. How did it taste?" Replied Teaff, "About like you'd expect a worm to taste."

CURLY LAMBEAU

Coach ■ Green Bay Packers ■ Dec. 11, 1978

As the second quarter ended in the championship game between the Packers and the New York Giants, Coach Curly Lambeau thought about what to say.

This would be one of the most important chalk talks of his career. With the Packers losing 16–14, the players counted on him for a revised game plan. The right strategy, adjustments, and words could turn the halftime deficit into a victory.

Incredibly, Lambeau never gave that all-important halftime talk. He got lost in thought on his way to the locker room and ended up lost in the stadium.

As the team headed for the locker room, Lambeau lingered behind his players and made a wrong turn under the Polo Grounds. He opened the door to what he thought was the clubhouse and wound up on the street. Before he realized his error, the door slammed shut behind him. The coach was locked out.

Lambeau pounded on the door, but it did no good. Then he raced to the nearest gate. The security guard refused to let him in. "If you're the coach, what are you doing out here on the sidewalk?" the guard sneered.

Lambeau hustled off to another gate and another guard. But no amount of pleas or threats could get him in there either. The second guard shoved him away, saying, "Yeah, sure, and I'm the King of England."

Meanwhile, back in the locker room, the Packers were wondering where their coach went. Back then teams didn't have an army of assistants like today's clubs do. As the halftime minutes went by, the puzzled players waited. They couldn't agree on a new game plan.

By this time, their angry, red-faced coach had charged the main gate, only to be stopped once again. Screaming at the top of his lungs, Lambeau attracted a big crowd, including some reporters.

The reporters recognized Lambeau right away. They convinced the guards that he was indeed the Green Bay coach. By the time he reached the locker room, though, the second half was about to begin. Without Lambeau's crucial halftime instructions, the Packers faltered in the last two quarters. They lost the championship 23–17.

WALLY BUTTS

Coach ■ Georgia Bulldogs ■ Oct. 26, 1946

Wally Butts was nicknamed "Weeping Wally" because he always told sob stories about his team's poor chances of winning. He even did it in 1946, when the Bulldogs went undefeated. Only once, in an ill-advised halftime pep talk that year, did he have real reason to cry.

Weeping Wally was in rare form that day in Greenville, South Carolina. His top-rated team was about to play hapless Furman University. He had already told the press that the Bulldogs were crippled by injuries. He claimed they were in no condition to be playing Furman. One local reporter actually believed him and predicted an upset.

As usual, Butts was just blowing smoke. But he didn't want anyone to know that—especially his own players. The Bulldogs totally dominated the game, and led 28–7 at the half. But Butts read them the riot act in the locker room. "That's the sorriest exhibition of football I've ever seen," he railed. "Y'all ought to be behind 28–7 instead of ahead. It's just terrible."

Suddenly, Butts ran toward a fired-up, potbellied stove in the middle of the room and kicked it. The pipe connecting the stove to the ceiling broke loose. To Butt's complete dismay, a cloud of soot dusted him in black. Even worse, he hurt his foot so badly, he thought he had broken it.

"He's holding his foot and yelling at us, and we're

having to bite our lips to keep from laughing," recalled Porter Payne, a guard on the team. "Then he got so tickled at how absurd the scene was that he was about to burst out laughing, so he bit his tongue and limped out of the room."

Oh, by the way, Georgia won 70–7.

DEFENSELESS DEFENSES

*Some defenses are so weak they need se-
curity guards to protect them. Even the
Munchkins could knock them on their tails.
By year's end, they usually give up enough
ground to form a new continent. That's because their nickel defense isn't worth five
cents. For "The Weakest Defensive Performances," The Football Hall of SHAME inducts the following:*

CUMBERLAND COLLEGE

Oct. 7, 1916

No team ever suffered a more humiliating defeat than
Cumberland College. The team was crushed 222–0.

Blame the worst whipping in collegiate history on
poor field position. Cumberland had to play on the
same field with the Georgia Tech Yellow Jackets.

Tackling dummies would have put up a better defense. The losers were so powerless that the Yellow

Jackets scored on every single possession. Never before or since has a college team given up so many points (222), touchdowns (32), and yards (968) in one game.

Thirteen TDs came on returned interceptions, fumbles, punts, and kickoffs. Tech ran the ball only 29 times, but hit pay dirt on 19 of those carries. (Since the Yellow Jackets gained 528 yards on the ground, there was no need to pass.) Another 220 yards came on punt returns, and still another 220 yards on kickoff returns.

It was a mismatch even before the players put their uniforms on in Atlanta. Cumberland, a little school in Lebanon, Tennessee, had an informal pickup team. It was coached by a law student named Butch McQueen. Georgia Tech's powerful football program was run by the brilliant coach John Heisman—the man for whom the famous football trophy is named. Cumberland's team was a group of serious students who pored over textbooks. Tech's squad was made up of athletes who read mostly play books.

Cumberland found 16 students who were foolish enough to play Tech. One of them had played very little football, and joined the team just to take his first train ride. Unbeaten the year before, the Yellow Jackets viewed the game as an easy tune-up for the new season.

Wisely, the Cumberland officials wanted to call the game off. They realized that Napoleon stood a better chance at Waterloo than their team did at Tech's Grant Field. But an agreement had been signed between the two schools. The tiny college either had to play, or forfeit $3,000 in good-faith money. The school decided to risk life and limb rather than lose the three grand.

The scoreboard shows the worst slaughter in college history.
GEORGIA TECH ATHLETIC ASSN.

When the squad assembled for the trip to Atlanta, three players missed the train. They were either very smart or very lucky.

Although the Cumberland players didn't practice, they honestly believed they could play a decent game. They didn't expect to beat Tech. But they didn't expect the worst massacre in Atlanta since General Sherman sacked the city in the Civil War.

The turning point of the game came during the flip of the coin. Tech won the toss and chose to kick off. The play resulted in Cumberland's "first down." The quarterback was knocked down and out and carted off the field. He was the fortunate one. He didn't have to go through 2½ hours of agony like his teammates.

On the first play from scrimmage, Cumberland running back Morris Gouger plowed into the Tech line for a 3-yard gain. It was the highlight of the half for Cumberland. Unable to move the ball any farther, Cumberland punted. Tech's Everett Strupper returned the ball to the Cumberland 20-yard line. On the very next play, he scored a TD—one of eight he tallied that day.

On the ensuing kickoff, Cumberland fumbled the ball. Tech scooped it up and ran it in for a second touchdown. The drubbing had begun.

Trailing 28–0 midway through the first quarter, Cumberland came up with a new strategy. They decided they would be better off with the ball in Tech's territory. So Cumberland began kicking off instead of receiving after every Tech score. But the Yellow Jackets returned the first kickoff 70 yards and scored two plays later. The next kickoff was returned only 40 yards, but Tech hit pay dirt again anyway. This time, they scored on the first play from scrimmage. At the end of the first quarter Tech led 63–0. By halftime, that point total had doubled.

Heisman told his troops at the half to show no mercy. He said, "Men, we're in front, but you never know what those Cumberland players have up their sleeves. So in the second half, go out and hit 'em clear and hit 'em hard. Don't let up."

Heisman wanted to run up the score to prove a point. Back then, sportswriters often rated teams solely on how many points they scored. Heisman thought this was a poor way to judge the worth of a team. He chose the Cumberland game to show how easy—and meaningless—it was to beat a weak team.

Try as they might, the Yellow Jackets could tally only 96 points in the second half. The Tech backs were worn out from running up and down the field. Finally, Heisman let the tackles carry the ball. Thirteen players managed to score in the blowout.

Meanwhile, Cumberland had the offensive punch of a glassy-eyed boxer. The team's biggest passing play of the day went for 10 yards. But it didn't help much. The pass was thrown on third-and-28. Cumberland was unable to make a single first down. They rushed for minus 45 yards, completed 2 of 11 passes for a total of 14 yards, threw 4 interceptions, and fumbled 9 times.

One of those fumbles was a snap from center bungled by quarterback Leon McDonald. Pointing at the bouncing ball, McDonald shouted to backfield mate Morris Gouger, "Pick it up! Pick it up!" Gouger, beaten and weary from all the vicious tackling, saw the big Tech linemen crashing in. He yelled back to McDonald, "Pick it up yourself. It's your fumble."

Early in the fourth quarter, Heisman spotted an exhausted Cumberland player hiding under a blanket on the Tech bench.

"Son," said the coach gently, "you're on the wrong bench."

"Oh no I'm not," replied the pitiful player. "This is the Georgia Tech side, isn't it?"

"Yes."

"Well, then, this is the only place I'm safe. If I go back to my bench, I'm liable to get sent back in the game again!"

HOUSTON COUGARS

Nov. 23, 1968

Getting slaughtered 100–6 by the Houston Cougars certainly qualified the Tulsa Golden Hurricane for induction into The Football Hall of SHAME. After all, Tulsa had set a modern major college record by giving up 100 points.

However, Houston, not Tulsa, deserves the boos.

The City of Houston has a good reputation in medicine for saving hearts. But the Houston Cougars earned theirs on the football field for being heartless.

By the end of the third quarter, Houston led the injury-riddled, flu-stricken Tulsa Golden Hurricane 51–6. The visitors were totally outclassed. But Houston still wasn't satisfied.

The Cougars showed their meanness by rolling up a record 49 points in the fourth quarter.

The seed for the lopsided victory was planted a year earlier, in the final game of 1967. The Hurricane upset the visiting Cougars 22–13. That defeat cost Houston what would have been its first-ever Top Ten finish. Cougar coach Bill Yeoman left the field in a huff, refusing to shake hands with Tulsa coach Glenn Dobbs. "Wait until we get you back in our place next year!" Yeoman declared.

The next year, the Hurricane players knew they didn't have a ghost of a chance of winning. One of the nation's hottest teams, Houston was headed for an NCAA record for total offense. Tulsa, on the other hand, belonged in a hospital ward. Fifteen starters and a host of reserves were suffering from the flu. Four other first-stringers were out with injuries. The squad was in such bad shape there was talk of a forfeit. But the Hurricane players were too proud. They wanted to give it their all—which, unfortunately, wasn't very much.

Even so, Tulsa trailed only 24–6 early in the third quarter. But soon fever and fatigue began to take its toll, and the defense began to wilt. Yeoman, the merciless Cougar coach, wanted to run up the score and pad his team's offensive statistics. He kept his first string on the field until he had a 45-point lead going into the final quarter. Only then did he send in his fresh and eager second unit to carve up the weak and helpless Hurricane defense.

Houston made 7 fourth-period touchdowns. They had a 34-yard interception return, a 58-yard punt return, runs of 11 and 3 yards, and passes of 18, 26, and 27 yards. It was a tribute to the Astrodome scoreboard that it didn't blow a fuse.

Still, the Cougars didn't let up. With each touchdown, the 34,098 bloodthirsty homecoming fans demanded more. They kept screaming for 100 points and didn't shut up until their team obliged them.

Late in the game, Larry Gatlin (yes, the Larry Gatlin of country music fame), a reserve who didn't play enough to earn a varsity letter, caught a 27-yard touchdown pass. It was his only collegiate TD. That made the score 93–6 with a little more than four minutes left to play.

All Tulsa had to do was control the ball to avoid the ultimate indignity. Unfortunately, the Hurricane offense was just as pitiful as its defense. They decided to punt, but luckily, only 30 seconds remained. What more misery could happen in so short a time?

Here's what: Houston's Mike Simpson caught the punt on his 42-yard line and raced almost untouched all the way to the end zone. The Cougars point total was boosted to 99.

The chant from the crowd of "One hundred! One hundred!" was deafening. Placekicker Terry Leiweke, who complained he was getting leg cramps from kicking so much, stepped onto the field to try for his thirteenth extra point. The pressure was on, but he booted the ball through the uprights for Houston's 100th point. Leiweke was mobbed by his point-hungry teammates as the fans cheered.

At the end of the horror show, the Cougars had ravaged the sickly Hurricane for 37 first downs and 762 yards in total offense. They had scored 76 points in the second half for yet another modern NCAA record.

When questioned by reporters after the game, Yeoman denied he'd run up the score. Somehow, he was able to say this with a straight face. His counterpart, Dobbs, refused to shake hands after the game and said little to the press.

"No team deserves this kind of treatment," said Tulsa player David Moss years later. "To get beat and get your nose rubbed in it is the most devastating thing for an athlete.

"It was humiliating. I wanted to just hide under my bed and not come out for a year."

WASHINGTON REDSKINS

Dec. 8, 1940

The Washington Redskins suffered the most lopsided bout in pro football. The Chicago Bears clobbered them in an NFL championship contest 73–0.

The Redskins were beaten before they even set foot on the field. For that, they can blame their owner, George Preston Marshall.

Three weeks earlier, the Redskins had knocked off the Bears 7–3 after a questionable last-second call by an official. Marshall added insult to injury when he told the press, "The Bears are quitters. They're not a second-half team. They're just a bunch of crybabies. They fold up when the going gets tough." On December 8, Marshall choked on his own words.

As the Bears were ready to leave their locker room at Washington's Griffith Stadium, Coach George Halas handed them newspaper clippings of Marshall's remarks. "Gentlemen," said Halas, "this is what George Preston Marshall thinks of you. I think you're a great football team. Go out on the field and prove it."

They did.

Two and a half hours later, the Bears had racked up an awesome 73 points. To this day, that's the highest total ever in any NFL game. The Redskins had failed to score at all.

The fired-up Chicago team struck when the game was only 55 seconds old. Fullback Bill Osmanski skirted around left end and raced 68 yards for a touch-

down. The Bears tallied 21 points in the first 13 min
utes. They led 28–0 at the half. In contrast to Marshall'
opinion of them, the Bears didn't quit at halftime. I
the final 30 minutes, they scored 45 more points.

The Bears riddled the Redskins with a relentles
ground game. They kept them at bay with an over
whelming defense. Halas used all 33 eligible men on hi
squad. Fifteen of them scored. There was only on
question left in the second half. Would Chicago scor
more points on offense or defense? The Bears offens
piled up a total of 501 yards. Their defense picked off
Redskin passes, returning 3 for touchdowns.

Washington couldn't do anything right—and i
rubbed off on the public address announcer. With th
score 60–0, he displayed judgment and timing as poo
as the losers. He told the crowd, "Your attention i
directed to a very important announcement regardin
the sale of seats for the 1941 Redskin season." The fe
Washington fans still in the stadium broke their s
lence—with a round of boos. Then they lapsed bac
into a state of depression.

After Chicago's tenth TD, an official asked Halas
he would mind not kicking the extra point. The official
were down to their last ball. Too many had been boote
into the stands and carried away by fans. With a 60
point lead, Halas could be generous. He told his tea
to pass for the last two extra-point attempts. The
made one of them.

When the final gun sounded, one reporter in th
press box joked, "Marshall just shot himself!" In th
locker room after the game, Marshall didn't have muc
to say. His only comment was, "We needed a fifty-ma
line against their power."

Arthur Daley of *The New York Times* wrote: "S

one-sided was the match that press box critics could not single out any of the Redskin players for praise. There was no Redskin hero outside of Coach Ray Flaherty, who had to sit on the bench and absorb it all, too much a beating for so fine a gentleman and coach. At the end, the Redskin band played "Should Auld Acquaintance Be Forgot." If said acquaintance is the Chicago Bears, it should be forgot immediately.

In the quiet loser's locker room, reporters talked to Washington quarterback Sammy Baugh. They suggested the turning point of the game was early in the first quarter. Receiver Charley Malon had dropped a sure touchdown pass that would have tied the game.

"If Malon had caught that pass," a sportswriter asked Baugh, "wouldn't it have been an entirely different game?"

"Yeah," said Baugh. "The score would have been 3–7."

BOOING THE BOOSTERS

*Fans come to the stadium to watch a game
and engage in one of America's favorite pas-
times—booing. They boo at the whistle-
happy ref, the fumble-fingered runner, the
color-blind passer. But sometimes the real
boos shouldn't be directed at the field. They
should go to the stands. For "The Wildest
Behavior of Fans," The Football Hall of
SHAME inducts the following:*

THE SNOWBALLER

Denver Broncos Fan ■ Nov. 11, 1985

A dunderhead in Denver pulled a grandstand play that
cost the San Francisco 49ers a victory.

This fan threw a famous snowball. It was the first one
that directly affected the outcome of a professional
football game.

It was the end of the first half in Mile High Stadium.
The 49ers were about to attempt a 19-yard field goal.

78

The icy missile exploded on the field right in front of 49ers placeholder Matt Cavanaugh. It splattered a split second before he tried to spot the ball for kicker Ray Wersching. Rattled, Cavanaugh muffed the snap.

Unable to put the ball down for Wersching, Cavanaugh scrambled with it and lofted a desperate pass that fell incomplete. It was a crucial play because San Francisco lost to Denver by only one point, 17–16.

The Snowballer was part of a group of fans that thought flinging snowballs onto the field could help ice the game for their Broncos. They had already nailed 49er Joe Montana in the huddle. At one point in the game, side judge Bill Quinby lay sprawled on the ground after running into a player. The group showed their concern by pelting him with a barrage of snowballs.

At least fifty fans were ejected from the stadium for throwing snowballs during that Monday-night game. But only the Snowballer attained instant fame—and shame.

"It just happened on the spur of the moment," he confessed later. "Me and my buddy both threw snowballs at the same time. His hit the left upright [of the goalpost] and mine bounced in front of Cavanaugh."

Cavanaugh confirmed that the snowball had distracted him, causing the bobbled snap. "It landed right about the time the ball was snapped," he said. "It took my mind off the ball and I dropped it."

The snowball flew at least 35 yards, from Section 17 to the ground in front of Cavanaugh. But the Snowballer couldn't enjoy his accuracy. "Everybody around us started calling us jerks," he said. "That's when I realized it was stupid."

Just who would be that stupid? That's what *The San*

Francisco Examiner wanted to know. The newspaper offered $500 for the Snowballer to tell his story. He did, but would not reveal his name or accept the money.

"I'm really sorry about what I did, and I want to apologize to the 49ers and the 49er fans," he told *The Examiner.* "I don't want the money. I feel bad enough already. Everybody thinks I'm a jerk."

Can you blame them?

DONALD ENNIS

Baltimore Colts Fan ■ Dec. 11, 1971

Of all the fans who ever tried to snatch the ball during a game, Donald Ennis ranks as the most foolish.

He tried to steal the pigskin from one of the meanest men in pro football, Baltimore Colts linebacker Mike Curtis.

Ennis, who wore glasses, was a thirty-year-old lightweight from Rochester, New York. He was acting like a typical fan during a Colts home game against the Miami Dolphins. Suddenly, Ennis felt the urge to run onto the field and grab the football.

Anyone who valued life and limb knew better than to mess with Curtis. But Ennis must not have known why Curtis was called "The Animal." Hadn't Ennis heard the stories? The ones about how Curtis ate a windowpane of the team bus on the way to games? How he chewed the bars right off his face guard? The time during a practice scrimmage he beat up the opposing center—who just happened to be his roommate? And how he mauled his own quarterback, the great Johnny Unitas, in practice?

Fan Donald Ennis gets tackled by the Colts' Mike Curtis.
UPI/BETTMANN NEWSPHOTOS

It was obvious that Ennis was not an informed fan. With about three minutes left in the game, the Colts broke from their defensive huddle on the 40-yard line. Ennis left his end-zone seat and vaulted onto the field. He scooped up the ball and raced for the sideline. "What is going on here?" thundered Curtis.

The irate six-foot four-inch, 235-pound linebacker tore after the intruder. Catching up with Ennis, Curtis removed the ball from his hands—the hard way.

While 60,000 Municipal Stadium fans winced, Curtis swung his padded forearm. He whacked Ennis with a smash to the neck. In a game, the hit would have brought a 15-yard penalty for unnecessary roughness. "Welcome to the National Football League," Curtis growled. Ennis dropped the ball, and then dropped to the ground. He was unconscious.

Ennis was revived and taken to the hospital. Then he was taken to the Baltimore Municipal Court Building and charged with disorderly conduct.

After the game, Curtis said, "I believe in law and order. That fellow had no right being on the field. I felt it was in line to make him aware of his wrongdoing."

Ennis had plenty of time to think about his wrongdoing. He spent the next two weeks in bed, recovering.

IOWA HAWKEYES FANS

Nov. 24, 1905

Fans have often been loud enough to drive opposing teams batty, but no rooters topped Iowa's engineering students.

For rival Iowa State, the students tinkered all week to prepare a major surprise. On the day of the game, they carted out their prize noisemaker. It was an old steam engine with a piercing three-tone whistle.

Wearing cotton in their ears, the engineers set it up on the south end of the grandstand. Every time the Cyclones had the ball, they tied down the cord to the whistle. They blasted the daylights out of Iowa State.

The helmet-rattling blare was so loud that none of the Cyclones could hear the quarterback. He was forced to go from player to player shouting the signals. But that did little good. The racket disrupted their timing and broke their concentration. Needless to say, the whistle barely peeped when the ball was in Iowa's possession. Iowa won 8–0.

After the game, authorities confiscated the deafening noisemaker and it was never heard from again.

CALVIN COOLIDGE

President ■ United States of America ■ Dec. 7, 1925

If Calvin Coolidge had known as much about politics as he did about football, he never would have been President.

Our thirtieth president showed what kind of fan he was when he met Chicago Bears star Red Grange. Illinois Senator William McKinley had arranged for Coolidge to meet Grange, the "Galloping Ghost." No athlete was more popular at the time. Grange had been a star player for the University of Illinois. Then he signed with the Chicago Bears for an unheard of amount of money.

In 1924, Grange made college football history against the University of Michigan. In the first 12 minutes, he scored four times. He returned the opening kickoff for a 95-yard touchdown, and then scored on runs of 67, 56, and 44 yards. Later in the game he added another TD. It was one of the greatest performances of all time.

When Grange joined the Bears, he helped launch pro football to the heights it has reached today.

The day before he met Coolidge, 65,000 fans saw Grange play at the Polo Grounds in New York. He scored a touchdown and intercepted a pass as the Bears whipped the Giants 14–7. The game was covered by such famous writers as Grantland Rice, Westbrook Pegler, and Damon Runyon.

By now, everyone in America had heard of Red Grange. Well, almost everyone.

McKinley's limousine brought Grange to the White House. There, the senator introduced the football star to Coolidge. "Mr. President," said McKinley, "this is Red Grange of the Chicago Bears." Coolidge shook Grange's hand and said, quite seriously, "Nice to meet you, young man. I've always liked animal acts."

THE LEAPER

Boston Patriots Fan ■ Nov. 3, 1961

Most spectators are involved in the game. But one fan was too involved. He killed a team's chance for victory by deflecting a would-be touchdown pass. Worse yet, he got away with it.

It was in the closing moments of an AFL clash in Boston. The Dallas Texans (later the Kansas City Chiefs) were trailing the Patriots 28–21. The Texans tried to tie it up with a last-ditch flea flicker. The pass sailed 70 yards and was caught by Chris Burford. Fighting off three defenders, he fell on the Boston 3-yard line.

Thinking the game was over, thousands of eager Patriots fans ran onto the field. But the referees said there was time for one more play. The spectators were hustled off the field but allowed to ring the end zone. Somehow, one rabid rooter slipped unnoticed into the Patriot secondary.

Dallas quarterback Cotton Davidson fired a pass to Burford in the end zone. The ball never reached the receiver. Instead, the fan-turned-defender leaped into the air and tipped the ball away. The final gun sounded, and the fan disappeared into the cheering crowd.

In all the confusion, none of the officials spotted the fan's interference. None of the Texans did either, except for Davidson. But his cries of protest fell on deaf ears. Even his own coach, Hank Stram, wouldn't listen to him.

When the film of the game was developed, however, there was no dispute. The camera had caught the fan in the act.

No one knows for sure who the Leaper was. But, says Patriots spokesman Dave Loftis, with tongue in cheek, "The legend has grown around here that it was really [Patriots owner] Billy Sullivan."

CRUD DUDS

Some teams have proven that there truly is no accounting for taste. How else can you explain why certain squads run around looking like they just escaped from the circus? For "The Most Awful Uniforms Ever Worn," The Football Hall of SHAME inducts the following:

WORLD FOOTBALL LEAGUE

July 1975

In a wrongheaded attempt to add color to the game, melon heads in the World Football League office approved uniforms that would have made the teams look like fruit salads.

For the exhibition season, they decided to try color-coded pants. The idea was to help the fans identify various player positions. Apparently the WFL didn't think highly of its fans' intelligence.

In the test, pants of different colors would designate the positions of the players. Purple for offensive linemen, green for running backs, orange for wide receivers, blue for defensive linemen, red for linebackers, yellow for deep backs, and white with colored stars down the leg for quarterbacks.

When the fancy pants arrived for the Memphis Grizzlies, the players showed good taste. They refused to wear them.

Paul Warfield studied his orange trousers with the black vertical stripes for a long moment. Then he said, "I've spent eleven years in professional football trying to build a serious image. I'm too far along in my career to begin playing [famous clown] Emmett Kelly."

Added teammate Jim Kiick, eyeing his greenies, "I'd look like a lime tree—or some kind of fruit."

Larry Csonka simply threw the offending garment onto the locker room floor. He sneered, "Sure, and the coaches are going to wear shocking pink suits with high heels and those little lace caps they like so much. Heck, these pants are what the owners wear up in their air-conditioned suites when they watch the game. They figure it's only right that we dress as nicely as they do."

After the players informed the league they would not dress up like bananas, kumquats, and prunes, the league finally agreed to toss the uniforms.

Y. A. TITTLE

Cornerback ■ Louisiana State Tigers ■ Nov. 1, 1947

Y. A. Tittle was tackled by his own pants!

It happened in a key game against the visiting Mississippi Rebels. Tittle intercepted a Charley Conerly

Y. A. Tittle was tackled by his own pants.
LSU SPORTS INFORMATION DEPT.

pass in the second quarter at the LSU 15-yard line. The ball was meant for Barney Poole. Before Y. A. could make tracks for the LSU end zone, Poole grabbed hold of the back of Tittle's belt. As Tittle struggled to get free, his belt broke.

His Tiger-gold pants began a slow descent. But Y. A. took off anyway, holding the ball in his left hand and his pants up with his right. To his joy, Tittle saw an open field ahead of him. To his horror, he realized his pants were slipping lower and lower.

Suddenly, a Rebel closed in on him from the left side. Tittle switched the ball to his right hand. But when he went to grab his pants with the other hand, he was too late. His pants had fallen down! And so did he—at the LSU 38-yard line.

"If my pants hadn't fallen, I'd have scored easily," recalled Tittle, who put the moment behind him to become a star NFL quarterback and Hall of Famer.

"It was really an embarrassing moment. I kept asking my teammates to surround me, but they didn't help me a bit. They were all laughing so hard they couldn't do anything. Everybody was getting such a chuckle out of it except me."

The Tigers weren't laughing so hard when they realized that Tittle's pants cost them the victory. LSU failed to score on that series and lost the game 20–18.

"I was running for the winning touchdown, or at least to a spot where we could have kicked the winning field goal," Tittle said. "But we lost and Ole Miss went to the Sugar Bowl instead of us. Losing my pants kept us out of the Sugar Bowl. Imagine, I got tackled by my own pants."

PITTSBURGH PIRATES

1934

What owner Art Rooney did to his team was a crime. He put the Pittsburgh Pirates (who later became the Steelers) in striped jerseys that made them look like convicts.

The Pittsburgh Pirates look like convicts on a chain gang.
PRO FOOTBALL HALL OF FAME

"The uniforms were pretty bad," recalled Armand Niccolai, a tackle and kicker who wore the prison garb. "But since we had to buy our own shoes, helmets, and pads, we were just thankful to have uniforms."

Once the season started, however, their opponents really made them feel guilty. The Pirates would have played in longjohns to escape the razzing. "The other teams really got on us a lot about our uniforms," said Niccolai. "They called us 'the chain gang' and 'jailbirds.'"

Because of their silly suits, the Pirates can be pardoned for their lousy year. They finished the season with a dismal 2–10 record. The following year, the jailhouse jerseys were dumped. Said Niccolai, in a classic understatement, "Everybody was sure glad to see them go."

SAM McALLESTER

Fullback ■ Tennessee Volunteers ■ Nov. 24, 1904

In a game against Alabama, Sam McAllester added a clever but sneaky accessory to his uniform. He wore a wide leather belt with a leather loop sewn onto each side.

At first, the puzzled Alabama players couldn't figure out what the loops were for. But they found out midway through the second quarter of a scoreless game.

The Volunteers got the ball at midfield and ran the same play over and over. McAllester received the handoff, ran forward, and planted his foot on the back of a guard. Then his two backfield mates, the Caldwell brothers, each grabbed a loop of his belt and hurled him over the line. The play picked up at least five yards every time.

By tossing McAllester again and again, Tennessee drove down the field. They scored the game's only touchdown—when he was thrown into the end zone. Alabama had been thrown for a loop by McAllester's underhanded belt.

DENVER BRONCOS

1960–61

The Denver Broncos were the "laughing socks" of professional football. They wore hose with vertical stripes.

The ugly socks looked like they were stolen from a circus clown act. They were so comical that several players wanted to play barefoot. Others collected money to give to the owners for new socks—but their offer was turned down.

The socks went well with the uniforms the Broncos wore in their first two years in the AFL. General manager Dean Griffing had bought them at a bargain price, along with gross gold pants and brown jerseys. He got them from the former Copper Bowl.

The Broncos put up with two seasons of insults from opponents before they finally got relief. New head coach Jack Faulkner changed their colors to orange and blue. He also decided to get rid of the stupid-looking socks.

Faulkner knew it was something to celebrate, so he didn't just dispose of the hose. Instead, the coach held the Great Sock Barbecue, right before the opening of the season. It was at the club's practice field, and thousands of fans came. The players trotted around the field, holding up their hose. And then, as the crowd applauded, the socks were tossed into a huge bonfire. Nobody tried to hose them down.

RAH, RAH, RAH, HISS BOO BAH!

*There are some things the world could do
just fine without. War . . . famine . . . dis-
ease . . . four-legged team mascots. Who
needs them? Fans go to the stadium to
watch the game. If they want to watch ani-
mals, let the spectators go to the zoo. That's
where most of the mascots belong anyway.
Some of their stunts are so beastly, even the
ASPCA would put them away. For "The
Most Pathetic Performances by Mascots,"
The Football Hall of SHAME inducts the
following:*

SEAL

Mascot ■ University of Virginia ■ 1947–53

Seal was a lazy mutt. Only one thing inspired him at
games. During halftime, he would lift his leg on the
opponents' goalposts.

A black and white dog of uncertain breeding, he was
a legend in his own time. But he had a leg up on all

Seal was the University of Virginia's most famous mascot.
RALPH R. THOMPSON

other mascots in dampening the enemy's spirits. He did his most dubious deed at the University of Pennsylvania in 1949.

Seconds before the halftime gun, Seal headed for the Penn goalposts. But the Penn cheerleaders were prepared, and formed a line to block his path. Seal pondered the challenge for a moment. Then he made a beeline for the abandoned cheerleader bench—and lifted his leg on their megaphones.

Back on campus between gigs, Seal concentrated on his favorite pastime—partying. "It was a common sight to see this slow, bowlegged dog go home at night from some frat party," recalled John Herring, head of the school's student activity center.

The mutt died in 1953 from what a school official termed "overindulgence." More than 2,000 mourners attended his funeral. An antique black hearse bore his flower-draped casket, as a muffled roll of drums beat out the slow, somber "Death March."

Behind the hearse walked students, townspeople, and school administrators. Nasty, a mongrel who considered himself the heir to Seal's throne, also marched. He wore a black mourning band around one leg.

At the grave site, Dr. Charles Frankel, the team doctor, delivered the eulogy. He said in part, "I can see Seal now, leading the parade in a celestial stadium with golden hydrants and gilded megaphones at his disposal, megaphones such as the one at the University of Pennsylvania, where Seal passed his acid test with flying colors."

BEVO

Mascot ■ Texas Longhorns ■ 1916–present

As a mascot for the University of Texas, Bevo has been nothing but a lot of bull.

Actually, twelve different bulls have carried the sacred name of Bevo. The last two, Bevo XI and Bevo XII, lived up to the title of official school longhorn.

But the actions of the other ten have given Texas fans plenty to beef about.

Being a lazy cuss, Bevo I (1916–20) didn't serve too well as the school's mascot. He ended up getting served as a steak dinner at a large football banquet.

Next came the impostor—Bevo II (1932). He was a Hereford pretending to be a longhorn, but the Texas fans weren't fooled. They quickly spotted him for what he was, and retired him after one year.

He earned his share of shame, however, when he charged a Southern Methodist University cheerleader. She easily sidestepped him, and then bonked him over the head with a megaphone.

Bevo III (1945–48) didn't just bite the hand that fed him—he tried to crush it in a one-bull stampede. One day, he broke loose and terrorized the campus until being captured and hauled away for good.

Bevo IV (1949) was an ornery, red, 1,700-pound beast. In his debut, he battered a parked car before his handlers brought him under control. But after he leaped over an eight-foot fence, they realized he was just too much steer for them to handle.

The meanest Texas mascot of all was Bevo V (1950–

54). Fans often drove to the ranch where he was kept during the week just to see how he was doing. Sometimes they returned with cuts and bruises, or with ripped clothes. He was so strong he kicked down half the side of a barn.

In the lowlight of his career, he broke loose at a game, scattering the panic-stricken Baylor University marching band.

Bevo VI (1955–56) wasn't tough enough to be the school's mascot. The shouting and noise of the games scared him. Handlers often had to drag him onto the field.

One day, he ran right over the Rice University bench—trying to hightail it out of the stadium.

Nothing that exciting ever happened to Bevo VII (1957–65) and Bevo VIII (1965–66). They were rather dull and boring, so eventually they were turned out to pasture.

Bevo IX (1966–76) pretty much followed in their hoofprints, except for one quirk. He had this thing about women—he hated them. He'd just as soon stomp on them as look at them.

None of the Bevos were quite as shameful as Bevo X (1976–81). He didn't exactly make a fierce, unbeatable picture.

Since he couldn't cope with the excitement of each game, he was given mild tranquilizers. All he did then was stand around or lie down. Some disgusted fans hurled the ultimate insult, calling him Bevo the Cow.

It didn't help his image any when Texas running star Earl Campbell crashed into him in the end zone during a game. Campbell got up quickly after the collision.

But Bevo X, who had been lying down, stayed down.

SOONER SCHOONER

Mascot ■ Oklahoma Sooners ■ Jan. 1, 1985

When Oklahoma's pep squad brought their mascot onto the field sooner than they should have, it cost their team three points.

Early in the fourth quarter of the 1985 Orange Bowl, Oklahoma's Tim Lashar kicked a 22-yard field goal. It gave the Sooners an apparent 17–14 lead over the Washington Huskies. But a flag had been thrown on the play. Oklahoma was caught in an illegal formation. The resulting five-yard penalty negated the boot.

Oklahoma senior Rex Harris, however, didn't see the flag. Harris was the driver of the Sooner Schooner. That's the midget-sized covered wagon hauled onto the field by two white ponies after every Oklahoma score. The Ruf-Neks, a pep group in charge of the Schooner, directed Harris to go onto the field.

When he did, Harris didn't hear the cheers he expected. All he heard were the angry voices of the referees, who ordered the Schooner off the field. "As soon as we got on the field, the ref started yelling, 'Fifteen-yard penalty!' I had no idea what was going on," Harris recalled. He and the team quickly found out.

The Schooner's early entrance earned Oklahoma a 15-yard penalty for unsportsmanlike conduct. It was added to the 5-yard illegal procedure penalty. The two penalties added 20 yards to kicker Tim Lashar's field-goal try. His 42-yard attempt was blocked. The mo-

Sooner Schooner gets flagged for a penalty.
AP/WIDE WORLD PHOTOS

mentum swung toward Washington, which went on to win 28–17.

In 1986, Oklahoma returned to the Orange Bowl to play Penn State. Not wanting to take any more chances, officials docked the Schooner and kept it off the turf. It was bound to happen—Sooner or later.

GUMBO

Mascot ▪ New Orleans Saints ▪ 1967–present

For its capers, Gumbo the mascot has always belonged in the doghouse. Back in 1967, the New Orleans Restaurant Association gave the Saints a St. Bernard puppy. It was named after the city's famous stew.

Gumbo's job was to rally the fans and players from the sidelines. After four straight losing seasons, he ran away.

He was replaced by a female named Gumbo II. She once tried to help the Saints by chasing Pittsburgh Steeler quarterback Terry Bradshaw. He was scrambling for a touchdown when Gumbo II broke loose and tried to tackle him. (None of the Saints could do it.) Barking and snarling, Gumbo II tore after Bradshaw. He ran into the end zone for a TD. Then he sprinted even faster to the safety of the Pittsburgh bench.

After a while, Gumbo II couldn't cope with watching the Saints. By the halftime of each game, she would leave the sidelines. She'd go to the locked gate leading into the clubhouse and whine, bark, and scratch to be let off the field. She soon died of a stomach ailment. Apparently, said her owner, Larry Dale, "The Saints had made her sick to death."

Gumbo III knew right from the start that she wanted no part of the Saints. In her debut, she had to be dragged out onto the field. Then she curled up in a big lump and went to sleep. She repeated this performance at almost every game.

MAUDINE ORMSBY

Homecoming Queen ■ Ohio State ■ Nov. 12, 1926

Maudine Ormsby was the ugliest homecoming queen ever elected.

Maudine had a long, straight nose with wide nostrils, and big ears that she could wiggle. Her teeth were the size of piano keys. She had broad but bony hips, and bowed ribs. And was she fat! She stood only five feet tall and was just as wide. She weighed half a ton.

Maudine, you see, was a cow. The Ohio State student body elected a pure-bred, prize-winning Holstein as their 1926 homecoming queen.

The fraternities and sororities had all nominated their own candidates. But the independent students felt left out, and decided to put up their own candidate. They picked Maudine. She immediately gained the support of the College of Agriculture.

The university enrollment back then totaled only 9,000 students. But more than 13,000 ballots were cast—and the majority were for Maudine. (She beat out such write-in contenders as evangelist Aimee McPherson, Queen Mary, Helen of Troy, and entertainer Sophie Tucker.)

Some of her legitimate two-legged opponents protested the rigged election. But the homecoming committee decided to milk the prank for all it was worth. They allowed Maudine to wear her crown.

Maudine's chaperones wouldn't permit her to attend all the homecoming festivities. After all, she was only four years old. However, she did ride majestically in a horse-drawn float in the homecoming parade.

Unfortunately, Maudine failed to inspire the football team. It lost to Michigan—to the udder disappointment of Ohio State fans.

PENALTY PANDEMONIUM

Football is like a great book—Crime and Punishment. *The way some players try to get away with murder, you'd swear they lettered at prison. But, like most repeat offenders, they usually get caught red-handed. Referees have thrown enough flags at these criminals to cover an entire football field. For "The Most Outrageous Penalties Ever Committed," The Football Hall of SHAME inducts the following:*

WILLIAM "THE REFRIGERATOR" PERRY

Defensive Tackle-Fullback ■ Chicago Bears
Nov. 17, 1985

William Perry—Chicago's lovable, snaggle-toothed, 308-pound Teddy Bear—became the toast of America in his rookie year.

A defensive tackle who moonlighted as a part-time fullback, Perry was big news—in every sense of the word. His presence in the backfield as a runner, receiver, and blocker made him a national celebrity. It also made him a member of The Football Hall of SHAME—for the most outrageous illegal-use-of-hands penalty in pro football history.

It happened in the third quarter of a 44–0 blowout over the Dallas Cowboys. The Bears had a third-and-goal from the Dallas 2-yard line. Perry was sent in to the backfield to block for running back Walter Payton. When Payton received the handoff, the Fridge buried the first Dallas defender in his way. But other Cowboys had stacked Payton up at the line of scrimmage. So Perry took matters into his own massive hands. He picked Payton up like a picnic basket and tried to carry him into the end zone.

Perry should have known better. It's against the rules to aid a runner that way. He was flagged for illegal use of hands, a 10-yard infraction. The penalty pushed the Bears back to the 7-yard line. Later on, they settled for a field goal.

After the game, a teammate asked Perry, "What were you trying to do?"

"Trying to pick up the guy who was on Walter—and Walter, too," said the Fridge. "It was instinct. I just wanted to help my teammate. I didn't know you weren't allowed to do that." Ignorance of the law was no excuse. But in Perry's case, that's the way the rookie rumbled.

Payton, the NFL's all-time leading rusher, hardly needed Perry's help. But he said he "appreciated" Perry's effort, adding, "I'm just glad William didn't fall on me."

If Payton had crossed the goal line, he would have been the first player in history to score with a refrigerator on his back.

STETSON UNIVERSITY HATTERS

Nov. 12, 1947

When the Stetson Hatters blew their tops, they triggered one of the longest series of penalties ever called.

The Hatters were playing the Erskine College Flying Fleet in Due West, South Carolina. Erskine returned the second-half kickoff to its own 30-yard line. Stetson was called for clipping on the play. The refs advanced the ball to the Flying Fleet's 45-yard line.

When the angry Stetson players protested, the referee called a second penalty. This time the 15-yarder was for unsportsmanlike conduct.

The official moved the ball to the Stetson 40-yard line. Ewing and teammate Grant Wilbank started throwing fits. They pushed and shoved the refs. For that crime, the two were banished from the game. Even worse, the Hatters earned a third straight 15-yard penalty. Erskine now had the ball on the Stetson 25-yard line. Thanks to the hot-tempered Hatters, Erskine got there without running a single play.

The Hatters finally cooled down enough for the Fleet to run one play from scrimmage. It lost a yard. But before the Stetson players could cheer, the refs slapped them again—for unnecessary roughness. The ball was placed on Stetson's 11-yard line.

On the next play, the Flying Fleet scored a touchdown. Erskine's net offense was only 10 yards—though the record books show a 70-yard scoring drive. The other 60 yards came courtesy of the mad Hatters.

ANDY CVERCKO

Guard ■ Dallas Cowboys ■ Sept. 23, 1962

Andy Cvercko committed the most costly infraction in NFL history.

The result was that a dramatic 99-yard touchdown pass was turned into a shocking safety.

Of all times and places to be caught, Cvercko picked the absolute worst moment. Dallas was playing at home against the Pittsburgh Steelers. Losing 21–14 in the third quarter, the Cowboys had possession of the ball on their own one-yard line.

Cowboy quarterback Eddie LeBaron faded into the end zone and threw deep to wide receiver Frank Clarke. He caught the ball on the 45-yard line and scampered untouched into the end zone. It was an apparent 99-yard TD pass.

But the hometown fans' cheers turned to tears when they saw a flag thrown in the Dallas end zone. Cvercko had been caught holding Pittsburgh defensive lineman Big Daddy Lipscomb.

The play was called back. Then, to the amazement of fans, Cowboys, and Steelers alike, referee Emil Heintz signaled a safety for Pittsburgh.

Unknown to almost everyone except Heintz, a specific rule covered Cvercko's crime. Rule 9, Section 5, Article 2 stated: "It is a safety when the offense commits a foul and spot of enforcement is behind their goal line."

Instead of climbing to a 21–21 tie, the Cowboys now trailed 23–14.

"I never heard of the rule," admitted Steeler coach Buddy Parker. "But it was a good time to find out."

Dallas coach Tom Landry was also unaware of the little-known rule. He rushed onto the field in a rage and got into a heated argument with Heintz. The coach lost his temper, his voice—and some of his hair.

Meanwhile, the 19,478 fans in the Cotton Bowl began howling and booing in protest. After the free kick following the safety, Pittsburgh could not get a play off because of all the noise. In frustration, Steeler quarterback Bobby Layne pulled his team to the sideline. They stood there for about three minutes, until the fans calmed down.

Cvercko's penalty and the safety it caused were especially painful to the Cowboys. They lost the game by that 2-point margin, 30–28.

NORTHWESTERN WILDCATS

Nov. 8, 1947

Northwestern committed the most shameful series of penalties in college history, to turn sure victory into bitter defeat. And they did it after time had expired.

The Wildcats were hanging on to a slim 6–0 lead over the Ohio State Buckeyes. There was time for only one more play. The Buckeyes tried a last-gasp pass from Northwestern's 12-yard line. As the final gun sounded, defender Fatso Day intercepted the pass to secure the Wildcat win. Or so it seemed.

Noticing that Northwestern had twelve men on the field, the officials had thrown a flag. The Wildcats were penalized 5 yards. More important, Ohio State was given one more chance to score—this time from the 7-yard line. But Buckeye back Rod Swinehart was stopped at the 3-yard line. The Wildcats jumped up and down in celebration. Now they could claim victory. Or so it seemed.

Incredibly, the officials called Northwestern offside, granting Ohio State yet another shot at winning—even though the clock had expired. This time, the Buckeyes scored a touchdown on a pass from Pandel Savic to Jimmy Clark.

Now the best Northwestern could hope for was to block the point-after kick and settle for a 6–6 deadlock. Sure enough, Emil Moldea's conversion attempt was batted down. The Wildcats breathed a sigh of relief. At least they could walk away with a tie. Or so it seemed.

Unbelievably, the refs caught Northwestern offside again! Given another chance, Moldea kicked the extra point straight and true. The Wildcats trudged off the field knowing they had penalized themselves right into a shocking 7–6 defeat.

THE FUMBLE
FOLLIES

You can tell who they are by looking at their fingers—they're all thumbs. These clumsy bumblers carry the ball as if they have an allergy to pigskin. Their muffs often trigger a rash of boos and jeers that stay with them longer than the ball. For "The Wackiest Fumbles," The Football Hall of SHAME inducts the following:

JACK CONCANNON

Quarterback ■ Chicago Bears ■ Sept. 28, 1969

In one of the most embarrassing fumbles ever committed in pro football, Chicago Bears quarterback Jack Concannon coughed it up after calling time out.

The foolish fumble occurred in the first quarter of a game with the St. Louis Cardinals. The Bears had a first-and-10 at the Cardinal 34-yard line. In the huddle, Concannon told center Mike Pyle to snap the ball on a quick count. "Do it on the first sound you hear," said Concannon.

The teams lined up and Concannon took his place behind Pyle. Then he noticed that one of his teammates was not in position for the play. Concannon suddenly backed away, formed a T with his hands, and shouted "Time-out!"

But Pyle, being the good center that he was, followed orders. He snapped the ball on the very first sound he heard—even though it wasn't what he expected. The ball bounced off Concannon's knee and spurted 20 feet straight up. Like a shortstop racing in for a bunted pop-up, Cardinal linebacker Larry Stallings caught the ball on the run. He rambled 62 yards into the end zone for his very first career touchdown.

Nobody even chased him. Other than Pyle, all the Bears had obeyed Concannon's call for a time-out and didn't move. The play unfolded before the referee could react to the time-out.

The fumble was not only a letdown, but costly as well. It led to the touchdown that proved to be the margin of defeat. The Bears lost 20–17.

OAKLAND RAIDERS

Sept. 10, 1978

In the most shameful fumble in pro football history, the Oakland Raiders dropped the ball—on purpose. Then they batted and kicked it into the end zone for a game-saving touchdown.

"The play is in our playbook," bragged Oakland guard Gene Upshaw after the contest. "It's called 'Win at Any Cost.'"

With only 10 seconds left in the game, the Raiders

were desperate. Trailing the San Diego Chargers 20–14, Oakland really needed a touchdown. Raiders quarterback Ken Stabler took the snap at the San Diego 14–yard line. He looked for a receiver. Just as he realized nobody was open, Stabler was hit from his blind side. It looked like a game-ending sack.

But with a flick of his wrist, the crafty veteran fumbled the ball forward. It bounded to the 8-yard line, where Oakland's Pete Banaszak batted and booted it to the goal line. There, teammate Dave Casper took over. He kicked it into the end zone, falling on it for the tying touchdown. The point-after, which came after time had expired, gave the Raiders a victory. But they didn't deserve to win.

After the game, the three Oakland players admitted the fumble was a phony. "I tried to fumble," said Stabler. "If I get sacked, the game is over." Said Banaszak, "Sure I batted it. I could see a San Diego guy right alongside me. If I picked it up, he would have tackled me and the game would have been over." Added Casper, "Sure I helped the ball along into the end zone."

What the Raiders did was illegal, for sure. But the NFL said it was impossible for the officials to judge "intent." That's because Stabler, Banaszak, and Casper waited until the game was over to confess.

The NFL made certain the fake fumble didn't appear in any team's playbook the following year. They added a new rule that states: "Any fumble that occurs during a down after the two-minute warning may not be advanced by any member of the fumbling team, except the player who fumbled the ball."

EAST CAROLINA PIRATES

Sept. 13, 1980

It's nice to be kind, but the East Carolina Pirates were generous to a fault.

They kept giving away the football. In fact, they fumbled on five straight possessions in one quarter. It was a college record in botchery. They gave until it hurt. And all they had to show for it was a stinging defeat.

The Southwestern Louisiana Ragin' Cajuns were on the receiving end of the Pirates' charity. Highly favored ECU was leading 7–3 at the start of the third quarter. Then the team turned into gift givers.

Less than a minute into the second half, quarterback Carlton Nelson and running back Theodore Sutton bungled the handoff. They lost the ball on their 35-yard line. Six plays later, the Ragin' Cajuns had a 10–7 lead.

Nelson must have believed that one good turnover deserves another. He coughed the ball up again just three plays after the ensuing kickoff. Southwestern Louisiana recovered on the ECU 42-yard line and drove into the end zone. The score was 17–7.

The Pirates wasted little time handing out more goodies. On their third possession of the period, Nelson fumbled away the ball on the Ragin' Cajuns' 41-yard line. But the Cajuns couldn't exchange the gift for a score, and punted.

Two plays later, however, ECU gave Southwestern Louisiana another gift. Running back Mike Hawkins fumbled on his 20-yard line. The Ragin' Cajuns used that present to gain a 24–7 lead.

The Pirates' generosity knew no bounds. For the fifth straight possession, they turned the ball over. This time, a punt slipped through the hands of returner Willie Holley on the ECU 19-yard line. Southwestern Louisiana cashed that mistake in for a field goal. As the fourth quarter began, their lead had been widened to 27–7.

All but three of the Cajuns' points resulted from Pirate presents. Yet when the 27–21 victors walked off the field, they didn't even say thank you.

NEW YORK GIANTS

Nov. 19, 1978

The New York Giants were beating the Philadelphia Eagles 17–12, and only 28 seconds remained. The clock was running because the Eagles had used up their final time-out. The Giants faced a third-and-2 situation at their own 29-yard line. All they had to do was fall on the ball and the victory was theirs.

There was no way they could lose—except one. The possibility was totally farfetched. It couldn't happen. But impossible as it seems, it did.

The clock was ticking off the final seconds. New York's offensive coordinator Bob Gibson sent in the play "Pro 65 Up." The play called for fullback Larry Csonka to run over left guard. But most of the Giants in the huddle were stunned.

They yelled at quarterback Joe Pisarcik to change

the call and simply fall on the ball. They didn't want to take any chances with a missed handoff. It all made sense. Even if they didn't make the first down, time would run out before they had to run another play.

But Pisarcik had been reprimanded by Coach Gibson in the past for not following his orders. So he ran the play—or rather, attempted to run it.

Pisarcik took the center snap and pivoted to make the handoff. Then he lost control of the ball. It bounced off Csonka's hip and hit the artificial turf at Giants Stadium. Eagle defender Herman Edwards couldn't believe his eyes. He scooped up the loose ball and ran

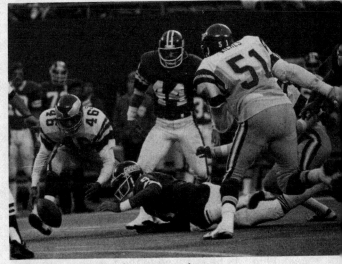

The ball and the game slip away from the New York Giants.
AP/WIDE WORLD PHOTOS

untouched into the end zone. With just 20 seconds left in the game, he gave Philadelphia an unbelievable 19–17 victory. New York head coach John McVay said, "That's the most horrifying ending to a ball game I've ever seen."

When the Giants lost the game, assistant coach Gibson lost his job.

DAVE SMITH

Wide Receiver ■ Pittsburgh Steelers ■ Oct. 18, 1971

A funny thing happened to Dave Smith on the way to an easy touchdown. He lost his self-control, his dignity, his sanity—and the ball.

It all happened on the most bungled spike ever watched by a national TV audience.

The Steelers were playing the Kansas City Chiefs on *Monday Night Football*. During the fourth quarter of the game (won by the Chiefs 38–16), Smith caught a pass from Steelers quarterback Terry Bradshaw. He broke through a crowd of defenders and zigzagged his way toward the end zone. Smith appeared to have a 55-yard touchdown reception.

But suddenly, he was struck with the urge to celebrate his feat. Smith raised the ball above his head in the opening gesture of the classic spike. Unfortunately, his timing was off. He was too eager to slam the ball to the turf. Smith failed to notice that he had yet to cross the goal line. As he streaked to the 5-yard line, the ball slipped out of his outstretched hand. It bounded all the way through the end zone.

The touchdown turned into a touchback. Because of Smith's dumb spike, the Steelers lost six sure points. Meantime, the Chiefs gained possession of the ball on the 20-yard line.

Adding to his misery, the Chiefs hooted and hollered as he ran past their bench toward his own.

He blamed his blunder on "tough luck"—but Smith was just plain out of luck.

MICHIGAN WOLVERINES

Nov. 22, 1969

It's one thing to drop the ball, but to drop your coach?

That's what the Michigan Wolverines did to their leader, Bo Schembechler.

It was one of the school's biggest games ever. The Wolverines faced their undefeated arch rival—and the nation's No. 1 team—the Ohio State Buckeyes. Michigan wanted revenge. Between 1954 and 1969 they had been beaten by the Buckeyes eleven times.

Schembechler psyched his players for the game. He made each one wear a tiny No. 50 on his jersey during practice. It was a subtle reminder of Ohio State's 50–14 rout over them the year before.

By game time, the underdog Wolverines were snarling. They attacked the Buckeyes with gusto all day. At the end, they trotted off the gridiron with a convincing 24–12 triumph. The Michigan players laughed it up and sang "Hail to the Victor." They waved red plastic roses, in reference to the trip they would make to the Rose Bowl.

The crowd of 103,588 at Michigan Stadium was roaring. Then the Wolverines lifted Schembechler onto their shoulders for the victory ride to the locker room. But incredibly, the players who performed so well on the field muffed the celebration. In one of the most embarrassing fumbles imaginable, they dropped Schembechler!

The unexpected fall aggravated an old football knee injury, but hardly hurt the coach's feelings. Recalled Schembechler, "It was the only thing those kids fumbled all day."

WOEFUL WINDUPS

Games, rivalries, seasons, and careers must all come to an end. Some finish gracefully. Others draw to a close without a shred of dignity. For "The Most Disastrous Farewell Performances," The Football Hall of SHAME inducts the following:

YALE BULLDOGS

Nov. 21, 1925

Yale has always been known for its students' high IQs. But the school's 1925 football team showed a total lack of brains in the final seconds of the year's biggest game.

Yale was only a yard away from the winning touchdown. Then the Bulldog backfield bickered so long over what play to run that time expired! It was a witless windup to a scoreless tie against arch rival Harvard.

Yale, the odds-on favorite to win big, totally dominated the game. The Bulldogs racked up 252 total yards and 13 first downs. Harvard managed only 106 yards and three first downs. But the Bulldogs also put on one of the greatest exhibitions of wasted opportunity ever seen on a college gridiron.

On five separate possessions, Yale had first downs inside the Crimson 10-yard line and failed to score. Twice the Bulldogs lost the ball on downs on the Harvard 2-yard line.

Yale played as though teamwork was a personal foul. They threw more cross words at each other than they did blocks against Harvard. Yale employed two shuttling quarterbacks. But they couldn't hold the team together long enough to drive over Harvard's goal. Throughout the first half, quarterback Dwight Fishwick squabbled openly with his backfield mates. They didn't want to run the plays he called.

The stupidest spat came during the final seconds of the 0–0 deadlock. Quarterback Phil Bunnell led Yale to a first down at the Crimson 5-yard line. Bunnell then sent Bruce Caldwell smashing into the line three straight times. The Bulldogs were within a yard of the promised land—and victory.

There was time for one more play. Yale could choose a field goal attempt or another plunge into the line. Instead, the backfield chose to fight—among themselves. Captain Johnny Joss quarreled with Bunnell over what play to run. As the dispute raged on, the last seconds ticked off the clock. No one had enough smarts to call a time-out.

Each team had scored zero—which, in the game's closing moments, was exactly the combined IQ of the Yale backfield.

PAUL "SKEETER" GOWAN

Running Back ■ Memphis State Tigers ■ Dec. 18, 1971

After clawing his way to a touchdown in the final game of his college career, Memphis State Tiger Paul "Skeeter" Gowan turned into a scaredy-cat.

It happened in the game against the San Jose State Spartans in the Pasadena Bowl, which the Tigers won 28–9. In the fourth period, the tiny Gowan skirted left end. He shook off two tacklers and scored an 18-yard touchdown.

Once in the end zone, Gowan slowed to a stop. But one burly and angry Spartan lineman kept right on coming. Gowan trotted out of the end zone. So did the lineman. Then Gowan heard his pursuer yell, "I'm gonna get you!" That was the little Tiger's signal to turn tail and run for safety.

"I could feel that heat coming right off him," Gowan recalled. "He wasn't going to stop, and I wasn't going to let him knock me into the stands, so I just kept on running."

The mini-Memphis ball carrier raced eight rows up into the end-zone bleachers. When he turned around, he saw—much to his relief—that the riled Spartan had finally given up the chase.

Gowan sat down, placed the ball in his lap, and caught his breath. Then he tossed the pigskin back to the ref—but didn't budge from his seat. "I stayed for about ten minutes," Gowan recalled. "I was in no hurry to get back down there and have that guy chase me again. After all, it was the last game I was ever going to play."

STANFORD CARDINAL VS. CALIFORNIA GOLDEN BEARS

Nov. 20, 1982

If this Stanford-California game had been a Disney film, the final play would have ended up on the cutting-room floor. It was just too goofy—even by Goofy's standards.

Stanford jumped ahead 20–19 on a dramatic field goal, with only 4 seconds left in the game. All the Cardinal team had to do to win was kick off and tackle the return man.

Kicker Mark Harmon purposely squibbed the ball. It bounced into the arms of California's Kevin Moen on the 43-yard line. Moen zigzagged upfield. Just before being hit, he tossed a lateral to teammate Richard Rodgers. Rodgers took the ball at the Stanford 48-yard line. As Rodgers was about to be tackled at the 44-yard line, he pitched the ball to Dwight Garner. Time had expired, but the play was still alive.

Garner was stopped. But before going down, he flipped the ball back to Rodgers. By now the field was filling up with people. Fans, players from the Stanford bench, and members of the school's band poured out onto the gridiron. They all thought the game was over. They were wrong.

Meantime, Rodgers was hemmed in again by Car-

**Kevin Moen races through the Stanford band
for a shocking touchdown.**
AP/WIDE WORLD PHOTOS

dinal players. He tossed the ball to teammate Mariet
Ford, who sprinted down to the 20-yard line. Then
Ford threw the ball blindly over his shoulder, praying
that another Golden Bear would catch it.

Sure enough, Moen, the player who had started it all,
was there. He snatched the lateral on the dead run at
the 25-yard line—next to the band's woodwinds. The
Stanford music makers unwittingly screened off poten-
tial tacklers. One Cardinal defender did chase Moen.
But he ran into the thick of the confused band members and eased off. Moen, however, kept threading his

123

way through the musicians, who began fleeing in all directions.

Moen dashed into the end zone. He sacked saxophonist Scott DeBarger and trampled trombonist Gary Tyrrell. It was the wildest ending ever to a football game. With no time left, California had used five laterals on a 57-yard kickoff return. They had turned certain defeat into an amazing 25–20 victory.

On the Stanford sideline, coach Paul Wiggin waited for an official to call the play back. But the only call made was "touchdown." The play left the Cardinal players wandering aimlessly around the field.

This was chaos. This was history. This was shame. "This was the biggest fiasco of all time," fumed Wiggin.

DENNY CLARK

Halfback ■ Michigan Wolverines ■ Nov. 30, 1905

Denny Clark suffered the saddest ending ever to a college football career.

His fuddle-brained blunder cost his team more than its first loss in five years. It also cost them the conference championship. Clark's goof was even worse because he had the bad luck to play football in an era when victory meant everything.

To Clark, all that mattered was winning. He couldn't stand for the highly favored Wolverines to lose to the University of Chicago Maroons in the Windy City. But the game had turned into a surprising defensive struggle. It looked like it would end in a scoreless tie—until Clark lost his head.

With five minutes left, Chicago punted into Michigan's end zone. Clark, a substitute halfback, fielded it as his teammates shouted, "Down it!" and "Stand still!" All he had to do was down the ball. According to the rules back then, Michigan would have had it on its own 25-yard line.

But Clark wanted to be a hero. He figured heroes don't play it safe. He quickly learned that boneheads don't either. To the shock of his teammates, Clark darted out of the end zone. He ran smack into two Chicago tacklers, who drove him back across his goal line for a safety. It turned out to be the only score of the contest.

Michigan coach "Hurry Up" Yost took Clark out of the game immediately. From that moment until he returned to the Ann Arbor campus the next day, Clark was sobbing. He could not be comforted. He couldn't face the other members of his team, even though they all assured him they weren't bitter. But apparently everyone else was.

Clark was avoided on campus and blasted by the press. One local newspaper headline read, "Clark 2, Michigan 0." Broken in spirit, he quit school a few days later.

Clark sought seclusion in a lumber camp in Michigan's barren north woods. There he lived like a hermit, brooding over the mistake that had wrecked his career. It took years to coax him out of his self-imposed exile.

WHO ELSE BELONGS IN THE FOOTBALL HALL OF SHAME?

Do you have any nominations for The Football Hall of SHAME? Give us your picks for the most shameful, embarrassing, deplorable, blundering, and boneheaded moments in football history. Here's your opportunity to pay a lighthearted tribute to the game we all love.

On separate sheets of paper, describe your nominations in detail. Those nominations that are documented with the greatest amount of facts, such as anecdotes, firsthand accounts, newspaper or magazine clippings, box scores, or photos, have the best chance of being inducted into The Football Hall of SHAME. Feel free to send as many nominations as you wish. If you don't find an existing category listed in *The Football Hall of*

SHAME that fits your nomination, then make up your own category. (All submitted material becomes the property of The Football Hall of SHAME and is non-returnable.) Mail your nominations to:

The Football Hall of SHAME
P.O. Box 31867
Palm Beach Gardens, FL 33420

THE WINNING TEAM

BRUCE NASH has felt the pain of football shame ever since he tried to play quarterback in a sandlot game in West Palm Beach, Florida. He called for the "Quarterback Fake, Fullback Take." The center was supposed to hike the ball through Nash's legs to the player directly behind Nash. Unfortunately, the center snapped the ball straight into Nash's stomach and knocked the wind out of him. Today, Nash collects memorabilia from the World Football League, and he still talks about the greatest game he ever saw—when Wichita State and his alma mater, Florida State, fumbled a record 27 times.

ALLAN ZULLO was an All-School-Yard receiver in Rockford, Illinois, where he was noted for his circus catches—he always looked like a clown. In high school, he tried out as a field goal kicker, but he was so bad he couldn't even split the uprights with an axe. As an expert on losers, Zullo is proud of his alma mater, Northern Illinois University, which did what no team had done against Northwestern in a record 34 straight games—lose. He has been rooting for the Tampa Bay Bucs ever since they dropped their first 26 games in a row.

BERNIE WARD, Hall of SHAME curator, grew up idolizing the Kansas State Wildcats, who have only recorded one winning season in the last 30 years. During his high school playing days in Norton, Kansas, Ward was known as "B.D."—because he was the team's blocking dummy. Ward still believes Roy Riegels ran the right way and that Cumberland College should bring back football.